YORK NOTES

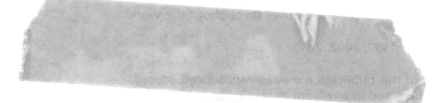

ROMEO AND JULIET

WILLIAM SHAKESPEARE

NOTES BY JOHN POLLEY

Longman
is an imprint of

PEARSON

York Press

YORK PRESS
322 Old Brompton Road, London SW5 9JH

PEARSON EDUCATION LIMITED
Edinburgh Gate, Harlow,
Essex CM20 2JE, United Kingdom
Associated companies, branches and representatives throughout the world

First published 1997
New edition 2002
This new and fully revised edition 2010

10 9 8 7 6 5 4 3 2 1

ISBN 978–1–4082–4882-9

Phototypeset by Pantek Arts Ltd, Maidstone
Printed in the UK

Illustrations by Alice Englander; Neil Gower (p. 6 only); and Bob Moulder
(p. 7, image of Shakespeare)

Contents

PART ONE
Introduction

Study and revision advice 5

Introducing *Romeo and Juliet* 6

PART TWO
Plot and Action

Plot summary 8

Act I 10

Act II 17

Act III 24

Act IV 31

Act V 36

Progress and revision check 40

PART THREE
Characters

Romeo 41

Juliet 42

Mercutio 43

The Nurse 44

Friar Lawrence 45

Benvolio and Tybalt 46

Lord Capulet 47

Paris 48

Progress and revision check 49

PART FOUR
KEY CONTEXTS AND THEMES

Key contexts...**50**

Key themes **51**

Progress and revision check **54**

PART FIVE
LANGUAGE AND STRUCTURE

Language **55**

Structure **58**

Progress and revision check **59**

PART SIX
GRADE BOOSTER

Understanding the question..**60**

Planning your answer **61**

How to use quotations..**62**

Sitting the examination **63**

Sitting the controlled assessment..................................**64**

Improve your grade...**65**

Annotated sample answers **66**

Further questions **68**

Literary terms..**69**

Checkpoint answers **70**

Study and revision advice

There are two main stages to your reading and work on *Romeo and Juliet*. Firstly, the study of the play as you read it. Secondly, your preparation or revision for exam or controlled assessment. These top tips will help you with both.

 ### READING AND STUDYING THE PLAY – DEVELOP INDEPENDENCE!

- Try to engage and respond **personally** to the characters, ideas and story – not just for your enjoyment, but also because it helps you develop your own, **independent ideas and thoughts** about *Romeo and Juliet*. This is something that examiners are very keen to see.

- **Talk** about the text with friends and family; ask questions in class; put forward your own viewpoint – and, if time, **read around** the text to find out about *Romeo and Juliet*.

- Take time to **consider** and **reflect** about the **key elements** of the play; keep your own notes, mind-maps, diagrams, scribbled jottings about the characters and how you respond to them; follow the story as it progresses (what do you think might happen?); discuss the main themes and ideas (what *do you* think it is about? True love? Courtly love? Society at war?); pick out language that impresses you or makes an **impact**, and so on.

- Treat your studying **creatively**. When you write essays or give talks about the play make your responses creative. Think about using really clear ways of explaining yourself, use unusual quotations and well-chosen vocabulary, and try powerful, persuasive ways of beginning or ending what you say or write.

 ### REVISION – DEVELOP ROUTINES AND PLANS!

- **Good revision** comes from **good planning**. Find out when your exam or controlled assessment is and then plan to look at key aspects of *Romeo and Juliet* on different days or times during your revision period. You could use these Notes – see **How can these Notes help me?** – and add dates or times when you are going to cover a particular topic.

- Use **different ways** of **revising**. Sometimes talking about the text and what you know/don't know with a friend or member of the family can help; other times, filling a sheet of A4 with all your ideas in different colour pens about a character, for example the different sides of Capulet, can make ideas come alive; other times, making short lists of quotations to learn, or numbering events in the plot can assist you.

- **Practise plans** and **essays**. As you get nearer the assessment time, start by looking at essay **questions** and writing short bulleted plans. Do several plans (you don't have to write the whole essay); then take those plans and add details to them (quotations, linked ideas). Finally, using the advice in **Part Six: Grade Booster**, write some practice essays and then check them out against the advice we have provided.

> **? DID YOU KNOW**
>
> *Romeo and Juliet* was one of the first half-dozen plays Shakespeare wrote.

Introducing *Romeo and Juliet*

SETTING AND LOCATION

Shakespeare chose Italy as the setting for a number of his plays. As far as we can tell, he never travelled abroad – but in his day Italy was regarded as a wealthy, romantic country where extravagant love affairs could properly be located. It is fitting that an immortal and tragic love story should take as its setting 'fair Verona' (Prologue 2).

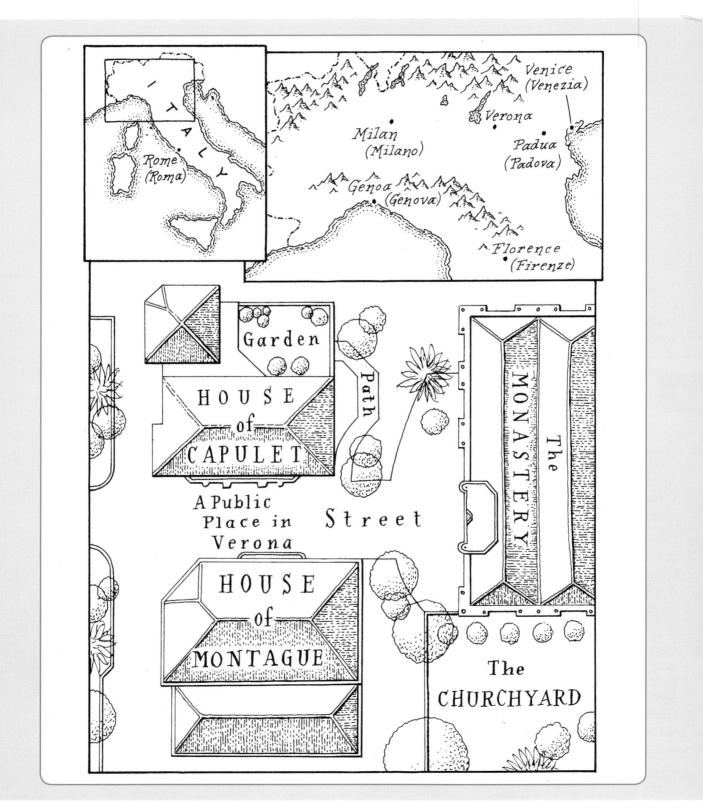

CHARACTERS: WHO'S WHO

LORD & LADY MONTAGUE
Romeo's parents

ROMEO
In love with Juliet

JULIET
In love with Romeo

LORD & LADY CAPULET
Juliet's parents

THE NURSE
Juliet's companion
since infancy

FRIAR LAWRENCE
Helps Romeo and Juliet

MERCUTIO
Romeo's friend
& kinsman to the Prince

TYBALT & BENVOLIO
Friends of Romeo

WILLIAM SHAKESPEARE: AUTHOR AND CONTEXT

1558 Elizabeth I becomes Queen of England

1564 William Shakespeare is baptised on 26 April in Stratford-upon-Avon, Warwickshire

1582 Marries Anne Hathaway

1588 Defeat of the Spanish Armada

1594 Joins Lord Chamberlain's Men (from 1603 named the King's Men) as actor and playwright

1595 *Romeo and Juliet* first performed

1599 Moves to newly opened Globe Theatre

1603 Elizabeth I dies on 24 March; James I, son of Mary Queen of Scots, succeeds to throne of England

1616 Shakespeare dies on 23 April, and is buried in Stratford

1623 First Folio of Shakespeare's plays published

PART TWO: PLOT AND ACTION

Plot summary: What happens in *Romeo and Juliet*?

REVISION ACTIVITY

- Go through the summary boxes below and **highlight** what you think is the **key moment** in each section.
- Then find each moment in the **text** and **re-read** it. Write down **two reasons** why you think each moment is so **important**.

SECTION 1: ACT I SCENE 1 – ACT II SCENE 2

Sunday

- *Morning*: The street fight. Romeo has been turned down by Rosaline.
- *Evening*: Paris asks Capulet if he can marry Juliet, Capulet's daughter.
- Romeo and Benvolio (members of the Montague family) decide to gatecrash the Capulets' masked ball and, together with Mercutio, arrive disguised outside the Capulets' house. Tybalt tries to pick a fight with Romeo.
- Romeo and Juliet fall in love instantly. Juliet discovers that Romeo is a Montague and therefore her enemy.
- *Night*: The balcony scene. Romeo secretly climbs into the garden of Juliet's house and they talk about their love for each other.

SECTION 2: ACT II SCENE 3 – ACT II SCENE 6

Monday morning

- *Daybreak*: Romeo asks Friar Lawrence to marry him and Juliet.
- *Morning*: Romeo hears that Tybalt wants a fight. He sends a message to Juliet asking her to come to the Friar's cell that afternoon.
- *Noon*: Juliet hurries to meet Romeo at Friar Lawrence's cell. The lovers leave with the Friar for a secret wedding.

Section 3: Act III scene 1 – Act III scene 4

Later on Monday

- *Afternoon*: Tybalt kills Mercutio and Romeo kills Tybalt. The Prince banishes Romeo from Verona with the threat of death if he remains.
- *Evening*: Romeo tries to kill himself, but is prevented by the Nurse. The Friar advises Romeo to spend the night with Juliet before leaving for exile in Mantua.
- Without consulting her, Capulet tells Paris he can marry Juliet. Juliet learns of Tybalt's death. She is desperate to see Romeo and the Nurse promises to find him.

Section 4: Act III scene 5

Tuesday morning

- *Before dawn*: After spending the night with Juliet, Romeo leaves for Mantua.
- *Morning*: Juliet refuses to marry Paris. The Friar gives her a potion that will make her appear dead for forty-two hours and thus prevent the marriage. They plot her eventual escape to Mantua.

Section 5: Act IV scene 1 – Act V scene 1

Later on Tuesday

- *Evening*: The wedding of Juliet and Paris is brought forward to Wednesday.
- *Night*: Juliet takes the drug.

Wednesday morning

- *Morning*: The Nurse discovers Juliet 'dead'.
- Friar Lawrence tells the Capulets to bring her corpse for burial.
- Balthasar, Romeo's servant, reaches Mantua and tells Romeo that Juliet is dead.
- Romeo prepares to leave for Verona.

Section 6: Act V scene 2 – Act V scene 3

Wednesday night – Thursday morning

- Friar Lawrence learns that Romeo thinks Juliet is dead, and rushes to the tomb.
- Beside Juliet's tomb, Paris and Romeo fight, and Romeo kills Paris.
- Romeo kisses Juliet for the last time and takes poison, just before Juliet wakes up from her drugged sleep.
- Juliet tries to kill herself by kissing Romeo's lips, then stabs herself and dies.
- As a consequence of the tragedy, the Montagues and Capulets make peace with each other.

DID YOU KNOW

You can find the complete works of William Shakespeare online.

Act I

Prologue: The scene is set

SUMMARY

❶ The Prologue briefly summarises what is to happen in the play.

WHY IS THIS PROLOGUE IMPORTANT?

A We learn that the story is to be about a **love affair**.

B The lovers are from **feuding** families.

C The feud ends with their **deaths**.

KNOWING THE STORY IN ADVANCE

The Prologue tells us the story in advance. This knowledge allows the audience an overview of the actions of Romeo and Juliet: we can see them struggling to attain happiness and know that they are always doomed to fail – in this life at least.

KEY QUOTE

'A pair of star-crossed lovers' (I.Prologue.6).

The Prologue tells us that the deaths of the 'star-crossed lovers' (line 6) is the only way that their 'parents' rage' (line 10) will end. Our knowledge of their certain death adds **pathos** to the events.

The Prologue takes the form of a **sonnet**, a characteristic form of love poetry that is also used elsewhere in the play.

EXAMINER'S TIP: WRITING ABOUT THE USE OF A SONNET TO INTRODUCE THE PLAY

You could draw attention to the use of a sonnet three other times in the play. For instance, the last fourteen lines of the play are a sonnet. This is a neat way to end the play, using the same form with which it started. These lines, however, are spoken by the lovers' fathers, with the concluding six lines given by the Prince to round things off.

Scene 1: Trouble on the streets

SUMMARY

❶ There is a fight on the streets of Verona.

❷ The fight is stopped by the Prince.

❸ Romeo's parents ask Benvolio where Romeo is.

WHY IS THIS SCENE IMPORTANT?

A A street fight breaks out between the feuding families, showing how **bitter** the dispute is.

B We see an **attempt** by one of the families to **stop** the fighting.

C The scene establishes the **state's concern** over the family feuding.

D We realise that it is to **Benvolio** that Romeo will tell his **true feelings**.

E Romeo reveals that he is desperately and miserably **in love**.

THE FEUDING FAMILIES

The running battle between the families establishes the notion of the family feud. Here the coarseness of the servants' language contrasts sharply with the purity of Romeo and Juliet's love affair. The appearance of the Prince brings the present fight to an abrupt end, but we know from the Prologue that there will be tragic consequences and that the love affair of Romeo and Juliet is to be played out against a background of hatred.

Tybalt's first appearance establishes him as one who enjoys a fight: 'Have at thee, coward!' (line 66), he challenges Benvolio. Romeo is absent from the fight, much to the relief of his parents. They are worried about his apparent depression and ask his best friend, Benvolio, to use their close friendship to discover what is the matter with Romeo.

ROMEO ALREADY IN LOVE

Romeo's fit of depression brought on by his unrequited love (for a girl called Rosaline) would have been perfectly understandable to Shakespeare's audience: love was meant to be a painful matter! Romeo is suffering from what is called **Petrarchan** love. Here the lover postures and displays lovesickness, while the object of his love adopts a cool and disdainful attitude towards him.

Romeo describes his feelings (lines 169–81) using **oxymoron** (e.g. 'cold fire') and **antithesis** ('Here's much to do with hate, but more with love'), which are typical of poems written in the Petrarchan tradition.

Benvolio is a good man, yet even he dismisses Romeo's strong feelings and suggests he look elsewhere for love. Benvolio's advice to look at other girls, 'Examine other beauties' (line 222), is naturally rejected by Romeo, though **ironically** it is precisely what is to happen.

EXAMINER'S TIP: WRITING ABOUT SOCIETY IN VERONA

You need to show how Shakespeare establishes that the purity of Romeo and Juliet's love is very much out of place in the violent and worldly-wise streets of Verona. Shakespeare often uses contrast to emphasise differences of moods, ideas and situations.

KEY QUOTE

'Out of her favour where I am in love' (I.1.162).

CHECKPOINT 1

What do Tybalt's first words reveal about his character?

★ **GRADE BOOSTER**

Think ahead! Shakespeare uses this scene to prepare us for much of what we will see later, such as Tybalt's aggressiveness and Romeo's unrequited love.

Scene 2: Juliet's future considered

Summary

1 Paris has come to Juliet's parents to seek her hand in marriage.

2 Capulet reveals that there is to be a masked ball tonight to which Paris is invited.

3 Romeo comes across the servant delivering the invitations and sees the name of the woman he loves – Rosaline – on the guest list.

4 He decides to go to the ball.

Why is this scene important?

A Juliet's father discusses with **Paris** his proposal of **marriage** to Juliet, but wants Juliet to **approve** it.

B We realise that Romeo and Juliet's **paths** are about to **cross**.

Marrying off his daughter

Paris discusses his proposal to marry Juliet with her father. It seems that Lord Capulet is reluctant to agree to an early marriage. Juliet's age would not, in those days, have ruled out her marrying, but Capulet feels his daughter is still a 'stranger in the world' (line 8) and would prefer her to marry when she is a couple of years older.

Paris's suggestion that there are younger mothers in Verona (I.2.12) is echoed later (I.3.62–3) by Lady Capulet, who reveals that she was married at a similarly early age herself.

Juliet is permitted a free choice of husband. Capulet is naturally keen that his daughter should find a considerate husband and agrees to Paris's proposal, provided that it meets with Juliet's approval. Later in the play his attitude has changed and he forces Juliet into the marriage.

> **KEY QUOTE**
>
> 'My will to her consent is but a part' (I.2.17).

The role of fate

Fate seems to take a hand by arranging that the servant with the guest list is illiterate. It therefore seems quite natural that he should ask for help in reading the names – and Romeo is there to provide it! This fortunate meeting gives Romeo the opportunity to go to the ball.

We remember from the Prologue that we are to witness the story of a 'pair of star-crossed lovers' whose love will be thwarted by the stars.

> **CHECKPOINT 2**
>
> How does Benvolio suggest that Romeo cure his unrequited love for Rosaline?

Examiner's tip: Writing about the way characters change in the play

You would point out how Capulet's attitude towards Juliet's choice of husband changes during the course of the play. In real life, people do change in all sorts of ways as they experience alterations in their lives.

Scene 3: Juliet's mother gives some advice

SUMMARY

❶ Lady Capulet discusses Paris's proposal of marriage with her daughter.

❷ The Nurse talks about her longstanding friendship with Juliet.

❸ Juliet agrees to consider Paris, but only if her parents approve.

WHY IS THIS SCENE IMPORTANT?

A We realise that Lady Capulet is **keen** for Juliet to marry Paris.

B The **friendship** between Juliet and her Nurse is established.

C We appreciate that Juliet is a **dutiful** daughter who will follow her parents' wishes.

LADY CAPULET AND JULIET'S MARRIAGE

Lady Capulet is far more keen than her husband for their daughter to marry. She herself was married young, so doesn't see Juliet's youth as a problem. The pressure Juliet is under later in the play to marry Paris may be initiated by her and this would account for her husband's apparent change of attitude towards Juliet.

Lady Capulet is rather impatient with the Nurse because she wishes to impress on her daughter that Paris's offer is a very attractive one. The desire for Juliet to marry comes across plainly in the blunt question 'How stands your dispositions to be married?' (line 58).

Lady Capulet's advice is very different from that given by the men: Juliet is not to compare Paris with anyone, but just to look at him very closely! The scene ends with Juliet excited at the prospect of the evening ahead and her mother fairly satisfied that her daughter will soon be married to a wealthy man.

> **KEY QUOTE**
>
> 'I'll look to like, if looking liking move' (I.3.90).

THE RELATIONSHIP BETWEEN JULIET AND THE NURSE

The closeness of Juliet's relationship with the Nurse is indicated by the description of how she was Juliet's wet-nurse and looked after her when she was a young child. Notice how the Nurse is prepared to go into quite intimate details of Juliet's upbringing.

The Nurse is excited at the prospect of Juliet marrying Paris. Her role is to be her young mistress's confidante, and we can readily understand why Juliet trusts her so completely.

> ★ **GRADE BOOSTER**
>
> Notice the strong contrast between the attitude towards Juliet of the Nurse and Lady Capulet.

EXAMINER'S TIP: WRITING ABOUT THE RELATIONSHIP BETWEEN JULIET AND THE NURSE

An interesting piece of writing would be to compare the first and last meetings of Juliet with her Nurse and describe the dramatic alteration in Juliet's attitude. You could comment on the closeness of the pair when we first see them, and then consider the way they have become totally estranged by the end.

Scene 4: The Montagues go to the ball

SUMMARY

❶ Romeo, Mercutio and the Montagues make their way to the ball.

❷ Mercutio speaks at some length about the need for Romeo to take a few risks.

❸ Romeo ends the scene expressing his misgivings about what might happen that night.

WHY IS THIS SCENE IMPORTANT?

A The Montagues come across as **high-spirited** young men looking forward to a good night out.

B Mercutio is depicted as a **good-humoured** young man looking for adventure.

C Romeo's **anxiety** that something **unpleasant** might happen is clear.

MERCUTIO'S IMPORTANCE IN THE PLAY

Mercutio's 'Queen Mab' speech is part of his tactic to persuade Romeo to enter into the fun of the evening. He describes the effect that Queen Mab has upon women, making them amorous. More importantly, Mercutio enables the audience to see that Romeo's attitude to his present love is nothing more than a pose: this matters, since Romeo is to fall truly in love with Juliet.

We immediately like Mercutio: he is lively, witty and pleasant. He has little chance to establish himself in the play, so this scene is a vital one, especially since it is his death that will force Romeo into a duel with Tybalt. We have to care about Mercutio, for otherwise his death would not seem worth avenging.

ROMEO'S PREMONITION

KEY QUOTE

'my mind misgives / Some consequence, yet hanging in the stars ...' (I.4.107–8).

Romeo's glum assertion that he feels something awful is about to overtake him (lines 107–12) echoes the reference to 'star-crossed lovers' in the first Prologue (line 6).

Romeo is not cheered up by Mercutio's banter. He is going to see Rosaline but has a feeling that something is about to happen that 'blows us from ourselves' (line 105), stopping him from seeing her. He asks the forces of fate to help him: 'But He that hath the steerage of my course / Direct my sail' (lines 113–14). Romeo fears that 'Some consequence, yet hanging in the stars' (line 108) may lead to his death.

EXAMINER'S TIP: WRITING ABOUT THE IMPORTANCE OF MERCUTIO

You could use this scene to show how Shakespeare gives Mercutio the chance to establish himself. Through his brilliant, evocative Queen Mab speech Shakespeare shows him to be an emotional and intelligent young man with a great deal of imagination and energy.

Scene 5: Romeo and Juliet meet

SUMMARY

❶ The scene opens with great activity as the final preparations are being made for the ball.

❷ Capulet gives a warm welcome to the guests.

❸ Romeo sees Juliet for the first time.

❹ Tybalt overhears Romeo describing the instant effect Juliet's beauty has upon him, and immediately wants a fight.

❺ Capulet is angry with Tybalt and tells him to behave himself.

❻ Romeo and Juliet meet and fall in love.

❼ They then discover that they belong to the rival families.

WHY IS THIS SCENE IMPORTANT?

A The **power** of Romeo and Juliet's **immediate attraction** is established.

B We see Tybalt's **dangerous rage** at the intrusion of a Montague on a Capulet family occasion.

C The discovery that the lovers come from **rival families** recalls the opening lines of the Prologue.

> **KEY CONNECTIONS**
>
> *Romeo and Juliet* has been used as the basis of three operas, by Bellini (1830), Gounod (1867) and Delius (1907).

CAPULET IN PARTY MOOD

The scene starts on a light-hearted note as Capulet offers a rambling welcome to his guests (lines 15–32). Romeo's response to Juliet's beauty is instant: she literally dazzles him, and this comes out in his language, e.g. 'O, she doth teach the torches to burn bright!' (line 44). By chance, Tybalt overhears Romeo's comment and reacts viciously.

Tybalt's response to Romeo's presence is important in the overall context of the play, as is the angry response Romeo receives from Capulet. He is obliged to leave the ball, swearing revenge. Capulet, however, wants nothing to spoil the atmosphere: after all, his daughter is about to meet the man he wants her to marry.

Ironically, Juliet does meet her husband-to-be that night – though it is Romeo, not Paris!

LOVE AT FIRST SIGHT

The meeting of the lovers has to be a sensation, and it is presented in a most unusual way. They dance together, and in their opening words they share a sonnet (lines 93–106). (This poetic form has also been used in the Prologue to the play.)

The sonnet has a beauty and formality which perfectly capture the awkwardness and power of the moment. The central image – of a pilgrim worshipping at a shrine – underlines the depth and purity of their love. The love they share is far from the Petrarchan version we have seen in Act I scene 1.

The discovery that they belong to rival families makes their love that much more ill-fated. Romeo, in particular, senses that his love for Juliet may have darker implications when he talks of the 'Prodigious birth of love' (line 140).

There is a grim truth in Juliet's view that her 'grave is like to be [her] wedding bed' (line 135). Juliet's reluctance to tell the Nurse which man interests her is a sign of her youth and shyness.

EXAMINER'S TIP: WRITING ABOUT THE LOVERS' FIRST MEETING

The vital thing to convey here is the beauty of the meeting of the lovers. We admire Shakespeare's cleverness in presenting this meeting in the form of a shared sonnet. The young couple are completely in step with each other at the very start. Remember, however, that Juliet is already aware of the danger that may lie ahead. Compare the mood of their first meeting with the 'balcony scene' in Act II scene 2.

KEY QUOTE

'My only love sprung from my only hate!' (I.5.138).

GRADE BOOSTER

Try summarising in note form every incident in this essential scene to help you revise.

GLOSSARY

Prodigious: monstrous

Act II

The Prologue: A quick update

Summary

❶ The Prologue describes the effect on Romeo and Juliet of falling in love with each other.

Why is this Prologue important?

A We realise Romeo has now forgotten his love for Rosaline and has fallen head-over-heels in love with Juliet.

Another love sonnet

By now we can appreciate how appropriate it is for the Chorus to use a sonnet to describe the progress of Romeo's love. Happily, and for now, the lovers are able to balance 'extremities with extreme sweet' (line 14).

Scene 1: Romeo is missing

Summary

❶ Benvolio and Mercutio are looking for Romeo after the ball.

❷ They are convinced that he is in love with Rosaline.

Why is this scene important?

A It establishes Romeo's **separation**, emotionally and physically, from his family and friends.

Benvolio and Mercutio's concerns

Romeo's friends still believe he is in love with Rosaline, and after a few coarse remarks decide that he does not want to be found since they have seen him climb an orchard wall.

Benvolio is more strait-laced in his language: he is concerned to find out his cousin's reaction to the ball. He has, after all, been charged by Romeo's parents with finding out his state of mind.

Mercutio is more than a little blunt with his sexual references. His view of the relations between the sexes contrasts sharply with the purity of the love vows so recently exchanged by Romeo and Juliet.

KEY QUOTE

'Blind is his love, and best befits the dark' (II.1.32).

EXAMINER'S TIP: WRITING ABOUT THE DRAMA OF THE FAMILY FEUD

This scene provides valuable evidence that for the Montagues a relationship with a Capulet is unthinkable. It is important that throughout the play such a relationship is considered impossible as far as the families are concerned. This little scene adds to the difficulties caused by Romeo and Juliet falling in love.

Scene 2: The balcony scene

SUMMARY

1. Romeo makes his way into Juliet's garden.
2. He sees her leaning over the balcony and hears her proclaim her love for him.
3. He tells her that he loves her.
4. Juliet is confused but delighted.
5. She asks him to arrange for them to be married.

WHY IS THIS SCENE IMPORTANT?

A The setting for the lovers' meeting is a **beautiful garden**.

B Juliet's **declaration** of love in an overheard soliloquy hastens the development of the love affair.

C We see that Juliet is very **practical**, telling Romeo that she will send the Nurse to him the next day to find out what he has planned.

THE DECLARATION OF LOVE

Just as Romeo had been dazzled by his first view of Juliet, so here in the opening lines she is described as a source of light (lines 2–22): she is 'the sun', outshining the stars 'As daylight doth a lamp'. The lovers are given plenty of time to make their vows before they are finally interrupted by a repeated call from the Nurse.

The lengthy farewell – Juliet comes and goes twice from the balcony – suggests the excitement that she is feeling and leads naturally into the often-quoted phrase 'Parting is such sweet sorrow' (line 184).

JULIET'S BEHAVIOUR

Juliet's declaration of love in the well-known soliloquy beginning 'Romeo, Romeo, Wherefore art thou Romeo?' (line 33) is a helpful dramatic device. It speeds up the action and frees Romeo to step forward, announce his presence and immediately declare his love too.

Juliet's first concern is for Romeo's safety (lines 64–5). Her next is that he may feel she is too forward (lines 85–106). This is very much what we would expect from a girl who regrets having shown her own feelings.

KEY QUOTE

'It is too rash, too unadvised too sudden' (II.2.118).

CHECKPOINT 3

What is the meaning of Juliet's phrase, 'Wherefore art thou Romeo'?

EXAMINER'S TIP: WRITING ABOUT SHAKESPEARE'S IMAGERY IN THIS PLAY

One of the key things you will want to bring out is the way in which different images of light (e.g. the moon and stars) are used to symbolise the nature of their love. Do you remember the very first lines of the play, in which the Prologue tells of a 'pair of star-crossed lovers'? We see the same idea here. You can also pick up this image in Act III scene 2 line 22.

Scene 3: The Friar agrees to conduct the marriage

SUMMARY

❶ Romeo goes to Friar Lawrence to ask for his help.

❷ The Friar expresses surprise that Romeo wishes to marry Juliet.

❸ He agrees to conduct the ceremony in an effort to unite the warring families.

WHY IS THIS SCENE IMPORTANT?

A When we see **Friar Lawrence** for the first time he is **collecting herbs**: a hint at future events.

B Romeo is prepared to put up with the Friar having a bit of **fun** at his **expense** in order to get the wedding under way.

C The Friar agrees to **marry** Romeo and Juliet because he believes that this may lead to a reconciliation between the families.

KEY QUOTE

'For this alliance may so happy prove / To turn your households' rancour to pure love' (II.3.91–2).

ASPECTS OF FRIAR LAWRENCE'S CHARACTER

The Friar appears with a basket of herbs that he has been picking. He is an expert in herbal remedies, and later we are able to believe that he has discovered a drug that will enable Juliet to appear dead.

Friar Lawrence expects Romeo to talk about his love for Rosaline. When he learns that Romeo has fallen in love with Juliet, he makes fun of him for his sudden change of affection from one woman to another. He suggests that 'Young men's love … lies / Not truly in their hearts, but in their eyes' (lines 67–8).

The Friar's decision to agree to marry the lovers is a no less sudden change!

The Friar is a respected figure in the play. His advice is sought by Romeo, the Nurse and Paris. This gives him a crucial position, as he sees it, in being able to unite the feuding families by a strategic marriage and so bring peace to the streets of Verona, turning their 'households' rancour to pure love' (line 92).

CHECKPOINT 4

What is the Friar's reaction to Romeo's news that he wants to marry Juliet?

KEY CONNECTIONS

Joan Lingard's *Across the Barricades* (1975) sets the Romeo and Juliet story in Northern Ireland during the Troubles in the early 1970s.

EXAMINER'S TIP: WRITING ABOUT THE FRIAR

This is our first meeting with the Friar, and you need to demonstrate how the Friar's actions later in the play are clearly signposted here. Is it just chance that he happens to be collecting herbs when we first see him? What else do we see in his behaviour here that will be important in the play?

Scene 4: The marriage details are agreed

SUMMARY

❶ Benvolio tells Mercutio that Tybalt has sent a challenge to Romeo.

❷ Romeo enters and there is some good-natured banter.

❸ The Nurse enters looking for Romeo.

❹ She tells Romeo that Juliet wants him to arrange their marriage.

WHY IS THIS SCENE IMPORTANT?

A We see the **consequences** of Tybalt's rage over Romeo's appearance at the masked ball.

B The warm **friendship** between Romeo and his male friends is clear.

C Although he has fun with the Nurse, Romeo is very **businesslike** in organising the details of the wedding ceremony.

TROUBLE IN THE BACKGROUND

We meet the Montague men discussing the events of the night before and considering what is to be done about Tybalt. Mercutio shows contempt for Tybalt (lines 20–36), indicating that if Romeo ducks the challenge, he at least will not.

Mercutio's coarse jokes about sex (again!) contrast sharply with the true love Romeo and Juliet have found. The entry of the Nurse gives Mercutio a new opportunity to make some personal comments. She is, of course, a member of the Capulet household and as such he sees her as a fair target for his rudeness.

The lovers are so blinded by their passions that they are unaware of the effect a relationship between them would have on their families. Shakespeare reminds us through the discussions of the Montague men that the feud remains a very serious matter.

ROMEO IN LOVE

Romeo is still having to put up with his friends' jokes about his romantic intentions, but he will not be deflected. The witty exchange between Romeo and his friends shows how much he has already changed from the miserable, lovesick young man we met at the beginning of the play. Benvolio underlines the change in lines 81–5.

Initially, Romeo is a little confused by the Nurse's apparent stupidity (lines 170–76), though he is purposeful and businesslike in ensuring that Juliet receives the correct message. Although the Nurse jokes with him he replies earnestly, determined that the wedding plans will be finalised.

KEY QUOTE

'Now art thou sociable; now art thou Romeo!' (II.4.81–2).

EXAMINER'S TIP: WRITING ABOUT LOVE IN ROMEO'S VERONA

It's a good idea to stress the contrast between the beauty of Romeo and Juliet's love and the aggressiveness of the background against which it is played out. The opening scene of the play introduces us to some very coarse young men looking for a fight and this scene reinforces that early impression.

Scene 5: The nurse gives Juliet the good news

SUMMARY

❶ The Nurse **torments** Juliet by not giving her the **news** that she wants straight away.

❷ The Nurse eventually tells Juliet that Romeo has **arranged** their wedding.

❸ Juliet is to go to **Friar Lawrence's cell** for the ceremony.

WHY IS THIS SCENE IMPORTANT?

A This scene, in which she is teased by the Nurse, helps to establish Juliet's youthfulness.

B The Nurse's teasing of Juliet also gives further evidence of the closeness between them.

KEY QUOTE

'O Lord, why look'st thou sad? / Though news be sad, yet tell them merrily' (II.5.21–2).

THE NURSE'S SENSE OF FUN

Juliet is waiting impatiently for the return of the Nurse, and this impatience gives an insight into the innocence of her nature. It also provides some amusement as the Nurse is deliberately evasive about Romeo's plans.

The Nurse enjoys the power that having this news gives. She pretends to be stupid, refusing to offer straight answers. Juliet reacts towards the Nurse in just the way Romeo did in the previous scene. The Nurse's delay in giving the news that Romeo has made the arrangements means that it is received with even greater joy.

The Nurse occupies a similar position in Juliet's life to the Friar in Romeo's. She enjoys her power over Juliet, as is illustrated by her teasing. The Friar, too, enjoys teasing Romeo, as we see earlier in this act. However, unlike the Friar, when things go wrong the Nurse lacks the courage to face the consequences of her actions, and instructs Juliet to marry Paris.

CHECKPOINT 5

Why is Juliet irritated by the Nurse in Act II scene 5?

EXAMINER'S TIP: WRITING ABOUT THE EXCHANGES BETWEEN JULIET AND THE NURSE

Why do you think the Nurse enjoys the power she has over Juliet? Does it make her feel more important, and that she has a special role to play? Is her love for Juliet genuine? The key to Juliet's impatience with the Nurse here is of course that she is young, head-over-heels in love and desperate to see Romeo again.

Scene 6: The wedding

SUMMARY

❶ Romeo and the Friar await Juliet's arrival at the Friar's cell.

❷ The young couple embrace.

❸ The wedding ceremony takes place off stage.

WHY IS THIS SCENE IMPORTANT?

A The Friar lectures Romeo on his **fickleness**, showing his enjoyment of the power he has over Romeo.

B The Friar's words **foreshadow** what is to come.

C The **symbolic** importance of **marriage** is stressed.

THE MARRIAGE CEREMONY

There is no celebration of the marriage on stage for, unlike a conventional love story, this tale does not reach its climax in the marriage of the young couple. The scene simply covers the last moments before the lovers are married.

The Friar's apprehensions about the suddenness of Romeo and Juliet's love, referring to 'violent delights' which have 'violent ends' (line 9), remind us of the words of the Prologue to Act I, and so have a double meaning here, foreshadowing future events.

The last fourteen lines of this scene amount to an exchange of vows between the two lovers. The dialogue lacks only the rhyme scheme to be a **sonnet**, although the final couplet goes to the Friar as he whisks them away to the (unseen) altar.

EXAMINER'S TIP: WRITING ABOUT THE DRAMATIC IMPORTANCE OF THIS SCENE

In most love stories the climax is the wedding, but here Shakespeare downplays the actual ceremony. Romeo and Juliet's marriage is important, but the play is really about their tragic deaths.

KEY QUOTE

'These violent delights have violent ends' (II.6.9).

KEY CONNECTIONS

Romeo and Juliet: Overture-Fantasy (1870) is a musical work by Tchaikovsky, based on Shakespeare's play.

 **DID YOU KNOW**

In modern productions of the play, this scene generally ends the first half.

Act III

Scene 1: The fatal fight

SUMMARY

❶ Benvolio and Mercutio are in the street discussing the possibility of a fight breaking out as Tybalt enters, looking for Romeo.

❷ Romeo enters. Tybalt insults him, but Romeo tries to keep things peaceful. This enrages Mercutio, who starts to fight Tybalt.

❸ Romeo tries to stop the fight, but Mercutio is fatally wounded.

❹ Romeo is so infuriated by Mercutio's death that he now fights with Tybalt and kills him. Romeo flees.

❺ The Prince learns the details of the fighting from Benvolio. Romeo is sentenced to immediate banishment.

WHY IS THIS SCENE IMPORTANT?

A This scene shows where the **violence** briefly seen in Act I scene 1 can lead to when men are ruled by **prejudice** and the desire for **revenge**.

B We see Romeo torn between his new-found **love** for the Capulets and his **fear** that he will be thought less than a man if he is not prepared to **avenge** his friend's death.

C The scene provides evidence of how **rage** can turn a **peace-loving** man into a **killer**, as Romeo kills Tybalt.

D It is at this point in the play that events finally **turn against** Romeo.

> **KEY QUOTE**
>
> 'Thy beauty hath made me effeminate, / And in my temper softened valour's steel!' (III.1.110–11).

THE FEUD REACHES ITS CLIMAX

The events of this scene are fast-paced and violent. It is a hot day, and the men of both households are out looking for trouble. Just as in Act I scene 1, Benvolio is playing the role of peacemaker and trying to persuade Mercutio to go home and avoid trouble. Mercutio, as usual, will not listen.

Mercutio is on the point of fighting with Tybalt when Romeo arrives from the wedding, and he is enraged by Romeo's reluctance to get involved. Mercutio's challenge to Tybalt as 'King of Cats' (line 74) recalls his earlier insult to him (II.4.19). Romeo tries to stop Mercutio and Tybalt fighting, but in the confusion Mercutio receives a fatal stab wound.

He dies in Romeo's arms with the haunting curse 'A plague o' both your houses!' (line 102) – a curse that is soon to be carried out. Mercutio's death effectively puts an end to the Friar's plan to simply reunite the warring families.

When Tybalt returns, Romeo feels that he must fight him both to avenge his friend Mercutio and to prove that his love for Juliet has not softened him. These feelings give his fighting an added power that is enough to beat Tybalt, yet even as Tybalt dies Romeo realises the consequences of what he has done: 'I am fortune's fool!' (line 132), he immediately declares.

Although we know that Romeo and Juliet are destined to die, we still hope that the workings of fate may be thwarted – but time and again, we are disappointed. This is one such occasion: just when everything is going so well, Romeo is caught up, against his will, in a series of events that shatter the happiness.

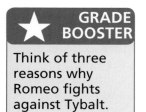

GRADE BOOSTER

Think of three reasons why Romeo fights against Tybalt.

ROMEO'S ROLE IN THE FIGHTING

Romeo is drawn into the fight much against his will. His marriage to Juliet has, in fact, started the reconciliation process between the two families. But two basic instincts – the desire of a man not to be thought a coward, and loyalty to his tribe – prevail, and Romeo is driven to fight Tybalt.

Tybalt in this scene and Paris in the closing scene of the play both die by Romeo's hand. We do not think of Romeo as a natural swordfighter, but on both occasions he is driven by strong motives which seem to give him the strength and skill he needs to defeat these men.

Furthermore, we know that he is fated to die for his love. His unexpected defeat of Tybalt seems to confirm that behind his actions fate is working.

EXAMINER'S TIP: WRITING ABOUT PRINCE ESCALUS

When writing about this scene, you might also like to consider the role of Prince Escalus. For a second time in the play, the Prince has to subdue the fighting and try to restore sense to the proceedings. The Prince has had enough of bloodshed so does not condemn Romeo to death. However, banishment is a severe penalty. He points out that 'Mercy but murders' (line 193), since it is no deterrent to wrongdoing. The sentence of banishment on Romeo leaves the possibility of a happy ending.

CHECKPOINT 6

Why does Lady Capulet object to the account of the fight that Benvolio gives to the Prince?

Scene 2: Juliet hears the news

SUMMARY

1. Juliet awaits the arrival of her new husband.

2. The Nurse enters, very upset to reveal that Romeo has been banished for killing Tybalt.

3. To calm her distraught young mistress, the Nurse promises to go to Romeo.

4. Juliet sends her ring, and asks the Nurse to tell Romeo to come to her.

EXAMINER'S TIP

Always plan your responses and write the plan in your answer booklet.

WHY IS THIS SCENE IMPORTANT?

A The **pathos** of Juliet's situation becomes immediately clear; she is married to her cousin's murderer.

B We see the Nurse acting almost **instinctively** to secure her young mistress's happiness. She agrees to fetch Romeo from Friar Lawrence so that the lovers can spend the night together.

KEY QUOTE

'Give me my Romeo! And when I shall die, / Take him and cut him out in little stars –' (III.2.21–2).

JULIET'S MISERY

Juliet is awaiting her new husband, unaware of what is happening elsewhere. She is eager for her wedding night to come, in contrast to Rosaline who will 'not be hit / With Cupid's arrow' (I.1.202–3) and showed only coldness towards Romeo.

Towards the end of the **soliloquy**, Juliet likens Romeo to a source of light, and then **ironically** suggests cutting him out 'in little stars' (line 22) when she dies. The opening Prologue's reference to a 'pair of star-crossed lovers' is ironically hinted at.

When Juliet learns from the Nurse that Romeo has caused the death of Tybalt, her confusion is shown in her use of **oxymoron**: 'A damnèd saint, an honourable villain' (line 79). Only when the Nurse shouts 'Shame come to Romeo!' (line 90) does Juliet rise to his defence.

Juliet's grief when she hears that Romeo is to be banished indicates the seriousness of the sentence of exile. She fears she may be 'maiden-widowèd' (line 135).

GRADE BOOSTER

What does the Nurse's admiration of the Friar suggest about her – and him?

EXAMINER'S TIP: WRITING ABOUT THE CLOSENESS BETWEEN JULIET AND THE NURSE

The Nurse agrees to fetch Romeo to spend the night with Juliet, for the last time putting her love for Juliet before her own personal safety. This makes the Nurse's betrayal of Juliet – when it comes – that much harder for us to take.

Scene 3: The Friar proposes a rescue plan

SUMMARY

1 Friar Lawrence tells Romeo that the Prince has banished him for killing Tybalt.

2 Romeo responds that he might as well be dead.

3 The Friar tries to calm Romeo, who feels suicidal.

4 They are interrupted by the Nurse knocking at the door.

5 She tells them that Juliet is in the same state as Romeo.

6 The Friar brings some order to the scene by reassuring Romeo that not everything is lost. Romeo is to spend the night with Juliet then go to Mantua the next morning and await news from the Friar.

WHY IS THIS SCENE IMPORTANT?

A The full extent of Romeo's **misery** is developed in this scene.

B The Friar shows his ability to **think quickly** in organising a rescue plan for the lovers. He will be aware of the danger of his own position.

ROMEO'S MISERY

Romeo is in the Friar's cell unaware of the sentence passed on him by the Prince. When the Friar informs him of 'the Prince's doom' (lines 4, 9), Romeo's response to the news of his banishment echoes Juliet's moments earlier. He is given to sudden mood changes: he did, after all, fall violently in love with Juliet, so the violence of his reaction to being separated from her is consistent with his character.

The Friar's initial suggestion is that Romeo should put his trust in philosophy. As an older man, he is able to find solace in considering the eternal truths. This is not a great deal of comfort to a young man eagerly awaiting his wedding night!

THE FRIAR'S DILEMMA

The Friar feels responsible for what has happened and desperately seeks a way out of the dilemma. In fact, there is no real need for anyone to do anything at this stage; certainly Friar Lawrence will not be able to 'reverse a Prince's doom' (line 59). Time will pass, and Romeo may be forgiven. Then the couple will be able 'To blaze [their] marriage' (line 150).

On the other hand, it is the Friar who has made a tricky situation – two young people from rival families falling in love – an extremely dangerous one, by marrying the couple. It is in his interests to keep things as quiet as possible.

The Friar's scheme in this scene, for the lovers to communicate at a distance and wait for a change of social climate in Verona, seems quite plausible. However, the plan relies on things going on predictably, and so far in the story nothing has worked out that way.

EXAMINER'S TIP: WRITING ABOUT ROMEO'S REACTIONS TO BANISHMENT

In writing about this scene, you should try to show how the violence of Romeo's reaction to his banishment more or less forces the Friar to take action. Romeo's reaction also helps us to understand a little more clearly the sort of man he is – and why he falls so quickly and deeply in love with Juliet.

GRADE BOOSTER

Note how Romeo's words 'In what vile part of this anatomy / Doth my name lodge?' (III.3.105–6) echo Juliet's words on the balcony, 'What's in a name?'

EXAMINER'S TIP

Always read the whole examination paper before you start writing.

KEY QUOTE

'There is no world without Verona walls' (III.3.17).

Scene 4: The Capulet reaction to the death of Tybalt

SUMMARY

❶ The Capulets discuss with Paris the strength of Juliet's reaction to the news of Tybalt's death.

❷ They decide that her wedding with Paris should be arranged as soon as possible.

❸ Lady Capulet is told to give Juliet the message that the wedding will take place in three days' time.

WHY IS THIS SCENE IMPORTANT?

A The **sudden** decision of Capulet to insist that his daughter must marry Paris brings a new **urgency** into the story.

B Capulet is reverting to the **traditional** role of the father in a male-dominated society.

A HASTY MARRIAGE

Capulet abruptly abandons his earlier tolerance towards Juliet. He believes that she will agree to his 'desperate tender' (line 12) and marry Paris.

The discussion about Juliet's reaction to the death of Tybalt leads to the decision that the marriage will take place as quickly as possible – in the next seventy-two hours. It will be a quiet affair out of respect to the recently dead Tybalt, so that people will not think they 'held him carelessly' (line 25).

Arrangements for the hasty marriage are unobtrusively introduced but add to our sense of the pace of events. The audience feels the story is rushing towards a swift conclusion. The decision to force a quick marriage also rules out the solution just proposed by the Friar: that Romeo wait in Mantua until the social climate changes in Verona.

EXAMINER'S TIP: WRITING ABOUT CHARACTER DEVELOPMENT

One of Shakespeare's great strengths as a playwright is to show how people's characters are changed by events. At the beginning of the play, we were pleased to note that Capulet was not going to force his daughter into a marriage that she did not want. Events have changed his mind. It is also worth noting that Juliet had said that she would only marry a man who met with her parents' approval (I.3.90–2).

Scene 5: The lovers' parting

SUMMARY

1. The lovers are at the bedroom window, both putting off the moment of their final separation.

2. The Nurse arrives with news that Lady Capulet is coming to see Juliet. Romeo and Juliet part.

3. Lady Capulet greets the weeping Juliet with unexpected news of arrangements for the wedding with Paris.

4. Juliet refuses to cooperate.

5. Her enraged father gives her a final choice: marriage or disinheritance.

6. Juliet looks for guidance and comfort from the Nurse, who tells her to forget Romeo and marry Paris.

7. Juliet realises that only the Friar, to whom she is now going, can help her.

GRADE BOOSTER

Notice the extra power that comes from Juliet and Romeo both knowing that dawn has come – and knowing that the other person knows too!

WHY IS THIS SCENE IMPORTANT?

A There is great **poignancy** in the lovers' final farewell after just one night together.

B The Capulets put **impossible demands** on Juliet to marry, forcing her to take action.

C The Nurse's **advice** for her to **forget** Romeo effectively **ends** the **friendship** she shared with Juliet.

KEY QUOTE

'More light and light, more dark and dark our woes' (III.5.36).

THE FAREWELL

We skip the wedding night to concentrate on the lovers' final parting, in a passage of elevated poetry called an aubade. Juliet's spirits change dramatically in this scene. At the start, she feels loved and fulfilled. By the end, she has been deserted by everyone.

The final parting is staged in very much the same way as the balcony scene (II.2).

The position of the lovers during their final words (lines 42–52) also anticipates the last moments of Juliet's life (V.3), when she will be looking down on Romeo.

THE PARENTS' IMPOSSIBLE DEMANDS

The entrance of Lady Capulet brings an abrupt end to Juliet's grieving over her loss of Romeo as she is now hurried towards a marriage that cannot take place.

Lady Capulet's intended revenge on Romeo (lines 86–91) is very much like the Friar's scheme for the young man. Ironically, her plan includes giving Romeo a poison that will lead to his keeping Tybalt company in the grave.

Capulet enters, expecting the news of the early wedding to have cheered up Juliet, and his first words show sympathy for her supposed grief for Tybalt (lines 125–37). This is quickly replaced by an almost incoherent rage when he realises that Juliet will not obey him (lines 148–67).

Lady Capulet's response is predictably angry: right from the start, she has wanted her daughter to marry Paris.

CHECKPOINT 7

What do Juliet's final words to Romeo mean?

EXAMINER'S TIP: WRITING ABOUT JULIET'S BETRAYAL

Juliet is left with an ultimatum – marry Paris or be thrown out of the family. She turns to her remaining friend, the Nurse, for comfort. By the end of their conversation, however, Juliet knows that she is now alone. At the key moment, her faith in a loving father is dashed by his insistence upon a swift marriage to Paris. Betrayal by her remaining friend, the Nurse, leaves Juliet no option. 'Thou and my bosom henceforth shall be twain', she says (line 240). Juliet's one hope of salvation now is the Friar.

Act IV

Scene 1: Juliet turns to the Friar

SUMMARY

❶ At the Friar's cell, Paris seeks advice about his forthcoming wedding.

❷ Juliet arrives. Respecting her desire for privacy, Paris leaves.

❸ Juliet reveals the depth of her despair – she produces a knife and is ready to kill herself.

❹ The Friar proposes a scheme that she finds acceptable.

❺ Juliet departs with the drug, as the Friar writes a letter explaining to Romeo what is happening.

WHY IS THIS SCENE IMPORTANT?

A We notice the **parallel** between the behaviour of Juliet here as she consults the Friar and that of Romeo a short while earlier.

B The Friar once again appears able to sort things out. He **reassures** Juliet that all will be well and suggests a **plan** to save the situation.

THE CALMING APPROACH OF THE FRIAR

Juliet's conversation with Friar Lawrence is quite desperate and the Friar has to physically restrain her from stabbing herself to death. His approach to her misery contrasts with that of the Nurse. He is aware that a second wedding is impossible and that a practical solution is required.

He produces a 'vial' (line 93), containing the drug that will solve all the problems.

His scheme is far-fetched, but something has to be done. The Friar's plan is that tomorrow night, Wednesday, Juliet will drink a concoction that will make her appear dead for forty-two hours. She will be taken to the Capulets' burial vault.

The Friar will send a fellow friar with a message to Romeo in Mantua so that he can come to rescue Juliet when she wakes up.

THE FRIAR'S RESCUE PLAN

This is the third occasion on which the Friar's services have been used. He started by marrying the lovers (II.6), he went on to find a solution for Romeo's banishment (III.3), and now he is saving Juliet. He has to be very confident of his ability!

Now we understand why, on our first meeting with him, the Friar spent so much time discussing the plants he had picked. His knowledge of their various properties convinces us that this may be the eventual means of Juliet's salvation.

Yet we already know that things will go wrong, and we think that perhaps the drug will be the cause. In fact, the plan will go wrong for a far simpler reason: lack of communication.

KEY CONNECTIONS

The musical *West Side Story* is a modern interpretation of the play set in New York among rival gangs.

KEY QUOTE

'I long to die – / If what thou speak'st speak not of remedy' (IV.1.66–7).

Scene 4: The last-minute wedding preparations

Summary

❶ At three o'clock on the morning of the wedding day, Capulet and his wife are already up making final preparations.

❷ The Nurse is sent to rouse Juliet and 'trim her up' (line 24), as Capulet realises Paris has arrived.

Why is this scene important?

A This scene gives us a **glimpse** into what is going on in **another part** of the **house**.

B It provides an **ironic contrast** to the events we have just witnessed.

The Capulet household make preparations

This little scene provides a short break in the main action. The Capulets are still rushing around making preparations for the wedding that morning.

The family is happily and excitedly preparing for Juliet's wedding. The **irony** is that the audience knows full well that Juliet's recent actions, upstairs, are about to destroy this happiness.

Examiner's tip: Writing about the use of contrast

This scene also provides a stark contrast between the Capulet family's busy and happy preparations for the wedding, and the deep misery into which we know they will shortly be plunged.

EXAMINER'S TIP

The exam answer booklet contains enough paper for you to write all you need to get top marks!

Scene 5: Juliet's body is discovered

SUMMARY

① The Nurse is unable to wake Juliet, and discovers that the bride-to-be is apparently dead.

② Lord and Lady Capulet are overcome with grief.

③ Friar Lawrence and Paris are the last to arrive at the grim scene.

④ The family is engulfed in misery.

⑤ The wedding is transformed into a funeral as Friar Lawrence takes charge of the burial arrangements.

WHY IS THIS SCENE IMPORTANT?

A It sets the scene for the **final action** of the play.

B It shows that the **Friar's solution** – so far – is going according to **plan**.

DIFFERENT RESPONSES TO THE EVENTS

The reactions of Juliet's parents to her death are rather too poetic, though Capulet's words convey the shock he feels: 'Death lies on her like an untimely frost / Upon the sweetest flower of all the field' (lines 28–9).

The Friar's speech (lines 65–83) contrasts sharply with the expressions of grief all round him. He reassures Capulet that he should not blame himself for Juliet's death since the 'most [he] sought was her promotion' (line 71). To those unaware of the Friar's part in Juliet's 'death', his words would seem measured and reassuring; to the audience, they are obviously prepared.

Paris has little to say, but when he speaks he seems deeply upset by the loss of his beloved. The depth of his feelings for Juliet may not be obvious to the audience, whose focus is on the tragic love of Juliet and Romeo. Paris is, however, soon to die protecting what he sees as Juliet's honour.

EXAMINER'S TIP: WRITING ABOUT THE NURSE

It is the Nurse who discovers the dead Juliet and alerts the rest of the family to the tragedy. It is perhaps appropriate that the Nurse, who has betrayed Juliet, should be the one who has to break the dreadful news. The response of the Capulets seems rather overdone, particularly when you compare it to their reaction at the end of the play (V.3.202–7).

GRADE BOOSTER

Think about how an audience would be feeling at this point. Although we know Juliet is not dead it could be a powerful and moving scene, a 'rehearsal' for her actual death. Or is there some dark comedy here: are her parents getting what they deserve?

Act V

Scene 1: The exiled Romeo learns of Juliet's Death

SUMMARY

❶ Romeo is in Mantua.

❷ Unaware of the true situation, Balthasar has hurried from Verona to inform Romeo of Juliet's death.

❸ Romeo resolves to return immediately to be with her.

❹ He finds an apothecary who supplies him with a deadly poison.

WHY IS THIS SCENE IMPORTANT?

A The Friar's plan is beginning to go **wrong**.

B Shakespeare invites us to **contrast** the kindly Friar and the devilish Apothecary.

C Romeo is again portrayed as a **man of action**.

ROMEO'S STATE OF MIND

Romeo is sad and alone in Mantua. His opening soliloquy recounts a dream that prefigures what is to happen in this scene. It is in this depressed state of mind that he greets Balthasar who has just arrived from Verona.

His response to his friend's news, 'I defy you, stars!' (line 24), reminds the audience of the futility of what he intends to do. He is, after all, a 'star-crossed' lover (I.Prologue.6). His hastiness in dismissing Balthasar is followed by an equally hasty visit to an apothecary he has already noticed in Mantua. Violently, he demands poison from the unfortunate man for he is determined to 'lie with [Juliet] tonight' (line 34).

THE APOTHECARY AND THE FRIAR

The description of the Apothecary (lines 37–54) reminds us of the Friar, and suggests parallels between the two men. Romeo had noticed the Apothecary 'Culling of simples' (line 40), and while the Friar uses his understanding of herbs beneficially, the Apothecary uses his knowledge of drugs to bring a swift death.

Ironically, Romeo uses the poison to gain everlasting life with Juliet. Even more ironic is the fact that the revenge Lady Capulet seeks on Romeo for killing Tybalt is identical: 'an unaccustomed dram' (III.5.89–90).

KEY QUOTE

'Come, cordial, and not poison – go with me / To Juliet's grave, for there I must use thee' (V.1.85–6).

CHECKPOINT 9

What news does Balthasar bring to Romeo?

GLOSSARY

simples: medicinal plants

Both men provide drugs for Romeo and Juliet, which lead directly to their deaths. The Friar wants to do good but he effectively ends up supplying Juliet with a poison. The Apothecary supplies poison with the intention to kill. One is supposedly good, the other bad, yet the action of each leads to the deaths of the lovers.

Scene 2: The plan miscarries

GRADE BOOSTER

Make a note of the ways the Apothecary differs from Friar Lawrence.

SUMMARY

❶ Friar John brings Friar Lawrence the letter to Romeo that has not been delivered.

❷ Friar Lawrence dashes off to be with Juliet when she wakes from her drugged sleep.

WHY IS THIS SCENE IMPORTANT?

A We **learn** that Romeo and Juliet may still be **saved**.

FRIAR LAWRENCE HAS TO FACE FACTS

Friar Lawrence is quite content that his plans are working. The arrival of Friar John, the carrier of the vital message to Romeo that Juliet is not dead, alarms him; he realises the risks he is running since 'The letter was not nice' (line 18). At this stage he is content since he thinks the non-delivery of the vital letter only affects Juliet.

He thinks up a plan to avoid his part in the **tragedy** being revealed: he sends Friar John an 'iron crow' (line 21) to open the Capulet vault so that he can keep Juliet at his cell until Romeo is informed.

The reasons for Friar John being unable to deliver the crucial letter – he had been locked into a house where the plague was suspected – would be darkly comic if the consequences were not so grave.

The whole tragedy now hinges on a failure to deliver a letter. This seems a minor thing, but it really is a matter of life and death – the final piece of bad luck in the tragic love affair.

KEY QUOTE

'She will beshrew me much that Romeo / Hath had no notice of these accidents' (V.2.26–7).

When studying this scene, you might consider how big a part in the play is played by chance. Very often it is the smallest things – being in the wrong place at the wrong time or arriving a moment too soon or too late – that are the undoing of people's plans. There are so many apparently chance events in the story that you might end up thinking fate plays a considerable part in the lovers' lives.

GLOSSARY

nice: unimportant
crow: crowbar

Scene 3: The denouement

Summary

1. Paris is keeping watch over Juliet outside the Capulet family vault.

2. He hides when Romeo and Balthasar approach.

3. Having sent Balthasar away, Romeo breaks down the door to the vault.

4. Paris steps forward to challenge Romeo. They fight, and Paris is killed.

5. Romeo lays Paris beside the dead body of Juliet.

6. He looks at her corpse, takes the poison and dies 'with a kiss' (line 120).

7. Friar Lawrence arrives and meets Balthasar as Juliet begins to wake up.

8. The Friar hears the sounds of people approaching and tries to persuade Juliet to leave the vault.

9. Frightened for his own safety, the Friar runs off.

10. Juliet gazes at her dead husband. There is no poison left, so she takes Romeo's dagger and stabs herself.

11. The death of the lovers produces the grief that leads directly to the reconciliation of the Montagues and Capulets.

Why is this scene important?

A **Fate** drives the lovers to suicide.

B We see the **positive side** of **Paris** and the **negative** side of the **Friar**.

C The play ends on a vaguely **upbeat** note as the families are **reconciled**.

Romeo's behaviour at the Capulet tomb

Romeo's impetuous fighting with Tybalt had led to his banishment. The same passion drives him to kill Paris. At the end, it is all a matter of timing: Romeo kills himself just before Juliet wakes up from her drugged sleep.

Romeo's farewell speech to Juliet (lines 88–120) provides a beautiful conclusion to the love affair. The speech echoes that given by Juliet before she falls unconscious (IV.3).

Friar Lawrence's conduct

The Friar realises that his entire plan has crumbled and he faces public disgrace. His suggestion that Juliet should retire to a 'sisterhood of holy nuns' (line 157) seems remarkably cowardly. It would remove her from public view, but to a young woman who has just lost her husband it might not seem the ideal solution.

The Friar is over-hasty in abandoning Juliet, and she kills herself before anyone can enter the vault.

The Friar is allowed to speak, though his comment 'I will be brief' (line 229) introduces a speech that is thirty lines long! The Prince accepts the explanation and

GRADE BOOSTER

Pay careful attention to the Friar's behaviour in the last half of this scene.

reads the letter that Romeo had sent to his father. Turning to the surviving members of the feuding families, the Prince condemns them for pursuing their quarrels.

Despite all his errors and the clear evidence that the audience has of his guilty involvement in the events, the Friar is viewed favourably by the other characters. In a metaphorical sense, he has journeyed through mud during the course of the play – and emerged smelling of roses!

EXAMINER'S TIP: WRITING ABOUT THE END OF THE PLAY

The lovers are fated to die. Their deaths come as the result of tragic mistakes, chiefly those of people acting in haste. Romeo's rush of blood in Act III scene 1 leads to the death of Tybalt. Romeo reacts equally swiftly when he decides to return to Verona to be with Juliet. When challenged by Paris outside the vault, he does not hesitate but starts a fight that leads to the death of Paris. The Friar has the chance to save Juliet at least, but on hearing footsteps he panics and leaves her to her predictable suicide. Only at the end when five of Verona's finest young people have died is there time to consider the consequences of what has happened. The Prince points out that 'All are punished' (line 295). The 'parents' strife' (I.Prologue.8) is finally ended in the way the Prologue to Act I had warned us. We have come full circle.

KEY QUOTE

'For never was a story of more woe / Than this of Juliet and her Romeo' (V.3.309–10).

CHECKPOINT 10

What is the Prince's response to the Friar's account of what has happened?

Progress and revision check

Revision activity

1. Why is Romeo absent from the street fight at the start of the play? (Write your answers below)

   ....

2. Where does Romeo go after the Ball?

   ....

3. Whose death does Romeo fight to avenge?

   ....

4. What is Capulet's plan that causes Juliet to take the Friar's drug?

   ....

5. Why exactly does Romeo buy poison?

   ....

Revision activity

1. Why does Romeo decide to go to the ball in Act I scene 5?

   Start: *Romeo is infatuated with Rosaline at the opening of the play but various chance events lead him to meet Juliet …*

2. In what ways does the Friar's plan in Act IV scene 1 go wrong?

   Start: *Juliet is upset that she has lost Romeo and must marry Paris, and the Friar thinks up a desperate scheme to help her …*

Grade Booster ★

Show how the story is affected by unpredictable events.

Think about …

- The way chance meetings can change a character's fate
- The way unexpected things can alter a character's behaviour

For a C grade: Convey your ideas clearly and appropriately (you could use words from the question to guide your answer) and refer to details from the text (use specific examples).

For an A grade: Make sure you comment on the varied ways fate seems to play a hand in the events of the story and if possible come up with your own original ideas, perhaps exploring or questioning whether it *is* fate, or something more profound in the characters themselves, that leads to tragedy.

PART THREE: CHARACTERS

Romeo

WHO IS ROMEO?

Romeo Montague is the son of an important Veronese family. He is a serious young man, as much inclined to act with his heart as with his head, and completely committed to Juliet.

WHAT DOES ROMEO DO IN THE PLAY?

- He falls in love with Juliet at the ball (I.5).
- He proclaims his love for Juliet in the balcony scene (II.2).
- He marries Juliet (II.6).
- He kills Tybalt in a duel and is exiled (III.1).
- He returns to Verona unaware of Juliet's true state (V.1).
- He kills Paris and dies in Juliet's tomb (V.3).

CHECKPOINT 11

How is Romeo related to Benvolio?

HOW IS ROMEO DESCRIBED AND WHAT DOES IT MEAN?

Quotation	Means
'Verona brags of him To be a virtuous and well-governed youth.' **Capulet (I.5.67–8)**	He has a good reputation and is held in high esteem.
'Why, is not this better now than groaning for love? Now art thou sociable; now art thou Romeo!' **Mercutio (II.4.81–2)**	Romeo begins the play depressed and love-sick, but Juliet's love transforms and re-awakens him.
'O, I am fortune's fool!' **Romeo (III.1.132)**	When he rashly kills Tybalt in revenge he realises he has behaved stupidly and has lost control of his destiny.
'... I still will stay with thee, And never from this palace of dim night Depart again.' **Romeo (V.3.106–8)**	Romeo is loving, loyal and devoted to Juliet – so much so that he kills himself in order to stay by her side forever.

EXAMINER'S TIP: WRITING ABOUT ROMEO

Romeo enjoys being in love, even with the wrong woman. After having married Juliet, he seeks friendship with the Capulets. When Tybalt kills Mercutio, his anger propels him to kill Tybalt, an action he instantly and bitterly regrets. News of Juliet's supposed death produces a predictably violent reaction: he must kill himself. He finds poison and rushes back to Verona. Once there, nothing can stop him. He offers Paris the chance to escape but Paris dies, like Tybalt before him, a victim of Romeo's rage. Beside Juliet's body, Romeo swallows the poison.

Juliet

WHO IS JULIET?

Juliet Capulet is the daughter of the Capulets, the rival family to the Montagues. She is young, sensitive and resourceful, unafraid to give herself in love whatever the cost.

WHAT DOES JULIET DO IN THE PLAY?

- She meets and falls in love with Romeo at the ball (I.5).
- She proclaims her love for Romeo from her balcony (II.2).
- She marries Romeo (II.6).
- She spends a first and last night with Romeo (III.5).
- She takes the drug the Friar has supplied (IV.3).
- She wakes in the tomb and kills herself (V.3).

KEY CONNECTIONS

The actress Claire Danes played Juliet in Baz Luhrmann's 1996 film *William Shakespeare's Romeo + Juliet*. Watch the ball scene from the film and make notes on how Danes portrays Juliet.

HOW IS JULIET DESCRIBED AND WHAT DOES IT MEAN?

Quotation	Means
'… she doth teach the torches to burn bright! […] So shows a snowy dove trooping with crows, As yonder lady o'er her fellows shows.' **Romeo (I.5.44, 48–9)**	Romeo has come to the ball to see Rosaline but the beauty of Juliet outshines that of every girl there.
'Thou knowest the mask of night is on my face, Else would a maiden blush bepaint my cheek For that which thou hast heard me speak tonight.' **Juliet (II.2.85–7)**	Juliet describes her relief that the night covers her embarrassment in having declared her love. This shows her innocence, her youth and her sense of propriety.
'Death lies on her like an untimely frost Upon the sweetest flower of all the field.' **Capulet (IV.5.28–9)**	Her father's comment brings out the poignancy of Juliet's early death with this beautiful flower image.
'Is crimson in thy lips and in thy cheeks, And death's pale flag is not advancèd there.' **Romeo (V.3.95–6)**	Romeo looks upon his beautiful wife and almost ironically says he believes she is still alive as her beauty is still fresh and radiant.

EXAMINER'S TIP: WRITING ABOUT JULIET

Juliet's youth is a key factor in her **character**. She falls helplessly in love with Romeo and, reassured by his declarations in the balcony scene, she wants to marry him. Tybalt's death and Romeo's banishment leave her desolate. In desperation she turns to the Friar, but to make his plan work she needs enormous courage, as her speech in Act IV scene 3 (lines 20–58) demonstrates. When she awakes in the vault, we can be absolutely certain that she will choose to die beside her Romeo, so complete is her commitment to him.

Mercutio

WHO IS MERCUTIO?

Mercutio is one of the Prince's kinsmen and Romeo's friend, a lively, passionate man whose death in a duel with Tybalt fatally changes the course of Romeo's love.

WHAT DOES MERCUTIO DO IN THE PLAY?

- He accompanies Romeo to the masked ball (I.4).

- He attempts to cheer up Romeo who is suffering because of his love for Rosaline (I.4).

- He reveals that Tybalt has challenged Romeo (II.4).

- Embarrassed by Romeo's refusal to fight, he duels with Tybalt (III.1).

- Accidentally stabbed, as he lies dying he utters a curse on both the Capulets and Montagues (III.1.102–4).

HOW IS MERCUTIO DESCRIBED AND WHAT DOES IT MEAN?

Quotation	Means
'… You have dancing shoes With nimble soles …' Romeo (I.4.14–15)	Romeo contrasts Mercutio's light-hearted approach to life with his own sad state of mind.
'Peace, peace, Mercutio, peace! Thou talk'st of nothing.' Romeo (I.4.96–7)	Romeo is irritated by Mercutio's nonsensical babblings.
'O calm, dishonourable, vile submission! […] Tybalt, you rat-catcher, will you walk?' Mercutio (III.1.70–2)	Mercutio's rage at Romeo's apparent cowardice comes out in this violent challenge to Tybalt.
'… Brave Mercutio is dead! That gallant spirit hath aspired the clouds, Which too untimely here doth scorn the earth.' Benvolio (III.1.112–24)	Here Benvolio praises Mercutio's courage and grieves that he has died so young, showing how admired he was.

GRADE BOOSTER

Shakespeare shows Mercutio's spirit through the pun he makes on the word 'grave' even when he is dying: he is a 'grave man', i.e. a serious man, and about to die. Find other instances of puns in the play and think about what effect they have.

EXAMINER'S TIP: WRITING ABOUT MERCUTIO

A close friend of Romeo, Mercutio is an attractive character with an earthy sense of humour. When he and Benvolio are discussing Tybalt's challenge to Romeo, he doubts that the lovesick Romeo has the strength to take on Tybalt. He grows angrier as Romeo declines to duel with Tybalt. Finally, he can bear this 'vile submission' (III.1.70) no longer and is fatally wounded as Romeo tries to protect him. Mercutio's affection means so much to Romeo that we know he cannot help but seek vengeance for his friend's death. Now, a tragic conclusion is inevitable.

The Nurse

WHO IS THE NURSE?

The Nurse is Juliet's closest friend and confidante until the point at which Juliet is to be forced into marriage with Paris.

WHAT DOES THE NURSE DO IN THE PLAY?

- She is involved in the first discussions about Juliet's possible marriage to Paris (I.3).
- She reveals to Romeo and Juliet that each has met a member of wrong family (I.5).
- She is sent to Romeo to organise the marriage ceremony (II.4).
- She arranges for Romeo to come to Juliet after he has been banished (III.3).
- She unwisely suggests that Juliet marry Paris after Romeo has been exiled (III.5).
- She discovers the apparently dead body of Juliet (IV.5).

HOW IS THE NURSE DESCRIBED AND WHAT DOES IT MEAN?

Quotation	Means
'Go girl. Seek happy nights to happy days.' Nurse (I.3.98)	The Nurse is no prude: she knows that Juliet will enjoy the physical side of marriage.
To Romeo she is a 'good Nurse' and 'my dear Nurse'. Romeo (II.4)	Romeo likes the Nurse and is grateful for her part in organising their marriage.
'Ancient damnation! O most wicked fiend!' Juliet (III.5.235)	Juliet is utterly disgusted by the Nurse when her advice is to forget Romeo and marry Paris.
'Thou and my bosom henceforth shall be twain.' Juliet (III.5.240)	Juliet ends her friendship with the Nurse and is alone now in Verona.

CHECKPOINT 12

Why is the Nurse so close to Juliet?

EXAMINER'S TIP: WRITING ABOUT THE NURSE

The Nurse is Juliet's closest friend, which is hardly surprising as she has cared for Juliet since she was a baby. She is not particularly clever or sensitive, and early on she comes across as a comic figure. When Juliet falls for Romeo, the Nurse enjoys acting as Juliet's messenger. Later, she brings Juliet the shocking news of Tybalt's death and fetches Romeo from the Friar's cell. When the Capulets inform Juliet that she is to be married to Paris, the Nurse changes sides, praising Paris. Her last duty in the play is to be the one who discovers the supposedly dead Juliet.

Friar Lawrence

WHO IS FRIAR LAWRENCE?

He is Romeo's friend and advisor. He is respected by Romeo and has what may be called a sense of destiny, persuading himself that Romeo and Juliet's marriage will end the conflict between the Montagues and Capulets.

WHAT DOES FRIAR LAWRENCE DO IN THE PLAY?

- He agrees to marry Romeo and Juliet (II.3).
- He shelters Romeo after his fight with Tybalt and his banishment (III.3).
- He conceives a plan to help the lovers to reunite at some point in the future (III.3).
- He gives Juliet the drug to make her appear dead (IV.1).
- He is unable to stop Juliet killing herself (V.3).

EXAMINER'S TIP: WRITING ABOUT THE FRIAR

Friar Lawrence has a high opinion of his own importance, believing it is in his power to end the feud between the Capulets and the Montagues, and this impels him to marry Romeo and Juliet. In response to Juliet's plea for assistance in Act IV scene 1, he uses his knowledge of plants to help her. The herbs work, but the rest of the plan goes wrong. He hurries to the Capulets' vault to be with Juliet when she wakes up. When she refuses to leave the vault, he deserts her. Eventually he comes forward to reveal the truth. Therefore although he seems to have good motives, ultimately the Friar's mistakes have a part to play in the tragedy.

★ GRADE BOOSTER

Think about the similarities and differences between Romeo's relationship with the Friar and Juliet's relationship with the Nurse.

Benvolio and Tybalt

WHO ARE BENVOLIO AND TYBALT?

Benvolio and Tybalt come from rival families, but while Benvolio is pleasant and well-meaning, Tybalt is a constant trouble-maker.

WHAT DO THEY DO IN THE PLAY?

- Benvolio tries to stop the street fight (I.1.62–3).

- Tybalt insists on their fighting (I.1.64–6).

- Tybalt overhears Romeo at the ball: he has to be stopped from fighting him (I.5.54–92).

- Benvolio tries to avoid another fight (III.1) but Tybalt will not listen.

- Both men are dead by the end of this street brawl.

GRADE BOOSTER

Benvolio and Tybalt appear for the first time within seconds of each other in I.1.61–70. Note how different they appear from the start.

EXAMINER'S TIP: WRITING ABOUT BENVOLIO AND TYBALT

There is a marked contrast between the two men. Benvolio's name means 'I wish (or mean) well', and whenever we see him he is pleasant and well-intentioned, comforting Romeo in his unfulfilled love for Rosaline and trying to avoid conflict. Tybalt, however, is clearly set on fighting. He aggravates the fighting in the opening scene and causes the trouble in Act III that fatally changes the course of events. Tybalt represents the ugliness that lies just below the surface of society. If Verona is a divided society, Tybalt is one man who wishes it to remain so.

Lord Capulet

WHO IS LORD CAPULET?

Capulet is Juliet's father and at first is prepared to let her marry whom she wants, but he later changes his mind.

WHAT DOES LORD CAPULET DO IN THE PLAY?

● He wants to join in the street-fighting (I.1.69).

● He at first reluctantly discusses the possibility of Paris marrying Juliet (I.2).

● He later insists that Juliet marry Paris (III.5.125–95).

● After the tragic events, he seals the friendship with 'brother Montague' (V.3.296).

EXAMINER'S TIP: WRITING ABOUT CAPULET

His first appearance might suggest that he is a comic figure, but when we next see him he is seriously discussing Paris's possible marriage with Juliet. He seems quite a liberal father, allowing Juliet to choose whether or not she will marry Paris. After Tybalt's death, however, he is much sterner and insists on Juliet marrying Paris. He will not change his mind, and it is this decision that brings about the end of the tragedy.

GRADE BOOSTER

Think about the role Capulet plays in the plot. You could argue that to make the play more convincing Capulet has to become a stern father. His attitude forces Juliet to take the extreme measure of pretending to have died.

CHECKPOINT 13

Why does Capulet like the idea of Paris marrying Juliet?

Paris

WHO IS PARIS?

Paris is the young nobleman who wants to marry Juliet and for whom Capulet later arranges the marriage.

WHAT DOES PARIS DO IN THE PLAY?

- He discusses the possibility of marrying Juliet with Capulet (I.2).
- After Tybalt's death, Capulet revives his interest in the marriage (III.4).
- He courteously greets Juliet as she is about to visit the Friar (IV.1).
- He is killed by Romeo in the graveyard while he is guarding Juliet's tomb (V.3).

EXAMINER'S TIP: WRITING ABOUT PARIS

Paris plays a small but significant part in the drama. In a way, he provides a living example of **Petrarchan love**, the sort of love that Romeo has for Rosaline. Paris suffers throughout, never even getting a smile from Juliet. Despite that, he is prepared to guard her tomb – and, in fact, dies for the privilege, being killed in a short, brutal swordfight with Romeo.

GRADE BOOSTER

What is Paris's most important role in the play? Is it as a rival for Juliet's heart or perhaps in acting as a peacemaker? Note his opening lines, which show regret for the family feuding in Verona (I.2.4–5).

Progress and revision check

REVISION ACTIVITY

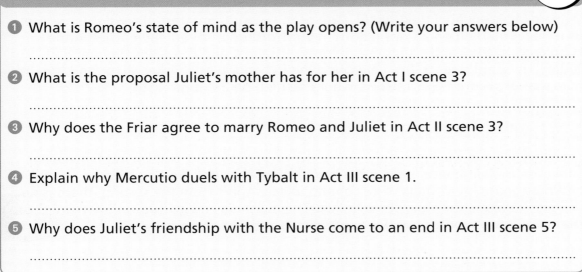

1 What is Romeo's state of mind as the play opens? (Write your answers below)

....

2 What is the proposal Juliet's mother has for her in Act I scene 3?

....

3 Why does the Friar agree to marry Romeo and Juliet in Act II scene 3?

....

4 Explain why Mercutio duels with Tybalt in Act III scene 1.

....

5 Why does Juliet's friendship with the Nurse come to an end in Act III scene 5?

....

REVISION ACTIVITY

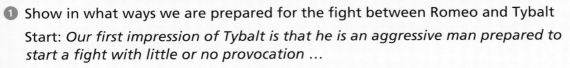

1 Show in what ways we are prepared for the fight between Romeo and Tybalt

Start: *Our first impression of Tybalt is that he is an aggressive man prepared to start a fight with little or no provocation ...*

2 What responsibility does the Friar have for the deaths of Romeo and Juliet?

Start: *The Friar has several reasons for assisting his friend Romeo to marry Juliet but ...*

GRADE BOOSTER ★

Why does Romeo fall in love with Juliet? Think about:

- Romeo's attitude to love and his disappointment over Rosaline
- Juliet's beauty and her readiness to commit herself whole-heartedly

For a C grade: Convey your ideas clearly and appropriately (you could use words from the question to guide your answer) and refer to details from the text (use specific examples).

For an A grade: Make sure you comment on the various ways Juliet is attractive to Romeo and if possible come up with your own original ideas. You could explore Romeo's general behaviour and actions too, and include an interpretation of what they tell us about him (and Juliet).

PART FOUR: KEY CONTEXTS AND THEMES

Key contexts

THE AUTHOR

William Shakespeare (1564–1616). One of the world's greatest playwrights, whose birthday is marked on 23 April. Born in Stratford-upon-Avon, he married Anne Hathaway in 1582 and had three children: Susanna, and the twins Hamnet and Judith. He spent twenty-five years working in London as a writer, actor and theatre manager. He retired to Stratford, where he died on 23 April 1616.

SETTING AND PLACE

The story is set in northern Italy, in the city of Verona, and, briefly, in Mantua. For Shakespeare's audience, Italy was a place where they believed murderous feuds and passionate love affairs were commonplace. Apart from the setting, there is no attempt to make the story seem Italian. The manners and attitudes shown are those that would commonly have been found in Elizabethan England.

THE FAMILY FEUD

In the Prologue we learn that Romeo and Juliet come from warring households in Verona. We are never told what their quarrel is about, only that it is bitter enough for a man like Tybalt to be always prepared to fight a Montague.

The instant attraction between the lovers immediately plunges them into the bitterness of family feuding. The perfectly natural love of a man and woman is made to seem wrong simply because they are trapped between two violently quarrelling families.

YOUNG LOVE

Juliet is fourteen, Romeo a couple of years older. Even with the different life expectancy of sixteenth-century Europeans, this was still rather young for marriage. Paris's interest in marrying Juliet (II.2) has a dramatic purpose, giving urgency to the story and even possibly forcing Juliet into considering marriage to Romeo on their second meeting.

The poem 'The Tragicall Historye of Romeus and Juliet' (1562) by Henry Brooke is generally accepted as Shakespeare's main source for the play. In this poem Juliet is sixteen years of age, and we may wonder why Shakespeare made his heroine younger. On the one hand, it makes her more vulnerable. On the other, it makes her transformation from a submissive child ready to give in to her parents' demands into a young woman prepared to fight and die for the man she loves more impressive.

KEY CONNECTIONS

Baz Luhrmann's film *William Shakespeare's Romeo + Juliet* (1996) is set in Verona Beach, Southern California. What effect does this modern setting have?

EXAMINER'S TIP: WRITING ABOUT SETTING AND PLACE

In most dramas the setting is important. In this play, it seems to be just a happy coincidence that the story should take place against the background of a beautiful Italian city. Try thinking about other possible settings for the play. Would the story still work set in Britain today?

Key themes

COURTLY LOVE

Our first meeting with Romeo shows us a stylised conventional type of love, sometimes called courtly (or Petrarchan) love.

This type of love is what grips Romeo in the opening scenes of the play: he sighs at Rosaline's lack of affection; he understands that she is not to be 'hit / With Cupid's arrow' (I.1.202–3), yet he is not able to forget her, nor is he prepared to try to do so. This is what makes him go to the Capulets' masked ball.

Yet once at the ball, Romeo's first words (I.5.41) reveal the immediate impact that seeing Juliet has upon him. This effect is even more astonishing considering that he feels he is madly in love with Rosaline. (See note on Paris, page 48.)

REVISION ACTIVITY

- Look at Romeo's speeches about his love for Rosaline in Act I scene 1 lines 202–31.
- Consider Benvolio's reaction to Romeo's speeches in that scene.
- Notice how Mercutio attempts to cheer up Romeo in Act I scene 4.
- See Paris's similar feelings when he is talking about Juliet in Act IV scene 1 lines 6–15.

EXAMINER'S TIP: WRITING ABOUT ROMEO IN LOVE

When writing about Romeo at the beginning of the play, it is important to stress that he really believes himself to be in love with Rosaline. This makes his sudden and complete transformation at the sight of Juliet that much more effective and significant.

CHECKPOINT 14

How often does Juliet meet Romeo?

SEXUAL LOVE

Another view of love is presented in the opening scene. This might be called sexual love, and throughout the play there are references to it. We first encounter it in the coarse humour of the servants in Act I scene 1.

It crops up again in our first meeting with the Nurse, when she jokes that 'Women grow by men' (I.3.88) and moments later is encouraging Juliet to view Paris sympathetically and 'Seek happy nights to happy days' (I.3.98). Mercutio's conversations frequently employ crude references that emphasise the physical relationship between the sexes.

KEY QUOTE

'Seek happy nights to happy days' (I.3.98).

REVISION ACTIVITY

- Look at the coarseness of the servants in Act I scene 1 lines 1–57.
- Study the conversation of the Nurse in Act I scene 3 when she is talking about love.
- Consider the crude sexual language used by Mercutio and Benvolio in Act II scene 1.
- Note the sort of language to which the Nurse is subjected in Act II scene 4.

TRUE LOVE

The popularity of the play does not lie in its different definitions of love but in its triumphant description of one love. The 'true love' of Romeo and Juliet shines out against the other types of love.

In the opening Prologue, the couple are described as 'star-crossed lovers' (I.Prologue.6) and on one level this suggests that their love is fated. On another level, the image of stars is appropriate as it captures the luminous quality of their love.

Romeo's first reaction to Juliet is that she lights up the room with her beauty (I.5.44). When he catches sight of her on her balcony, she is the 'light [breaking] through yonder window' (II.2.2). Juliet shares this view of their love. Initially, she is suspicious of the suddenness of the feeling, fearing that it is like lightning 'which doth cease to be / Ere one can say "It lightens"' (II.2.119–20). However, by the wedding night she believes her beloved Romeo will light up the heavens:

> … when I shall die,
> Take him and cut him out in little stars –
> And he will make the face of heaven so fine
> That all the world will be in love with night … (III.2.21–4)

> **KEY QUOTE**
>
> 'O, she doth teach the torches to burn bright!' (I.5.44).

REVISION ACTIVITY

- Note the use of the **sonnet** form at the beginning and end of the play, and when the lovers meet.
- Pick out five places where Romeo refers to Juliet as a source of light. Do the same for Juliet's references to Romeo.
- Is there evidence in Act II scene 6 that the Friar truly believes in their love?
- Look at the final lines in the play and make a note of the families' reactions.

EXAMINER'S TIP: THE LANGUAGE OF LOVE

In writing about the love affair of Romeo and Juliet, reference to the language used, in particular the sonnet form and the light **imagery**, is a clear indicator of a higher-performance candidate.

SOCIETY AT WAR

Apart from the different forms of love, the other main **theme** in the play is a society at war with itself: Romeo and Juliet's love is love against the odds. Romeo, we know from the very beginning of the play, has no business even to meet Juliet, a Capulet, let alone fall in love with her.

The masked ball is supposed to be the opportunity for Paris and Juliet to see whether they are suited to each other, yet into it comes an uninvited guest who ruins that plan. We are aware of the dangers all the time: the opening brawl, the bitterness of Tybalt, the perils of a Montague being discovered in the Capulet orchard, the street-fighting in the heat of the summer.

Against this background, a beautiful love forms, blossoms and becomes a lasting symbol of perfection. The strength of their doomed love has given the story of Romeo and Juliet its enduring popularity. Each generation sees Shakespeare differently and society's attitudes are always changing, but the power of love, the finest expression of the human spirit, remains constant.

GRADE BOOSTER

Make the connection between Tybalt's frustrated rage at the ball and Act III scene 1 where he is able to express his anger.

REVISION ACTIVITY

- Notice the ways the Prologue in Act I details the enmity between the families.
- The feuding comes back to upset Romeo when he is at his happiest (III.1).
- The families' conflict underlies Capulet's decision to marry Juliet to Paris (III.5).
- The resolution of the feud inspires the building of a monument to the lovers (V.3).

Progress and revision check

REVISION ACTIVITY

❶ Why is Verona a suitable setting for the play? (Write your answers below)

....

❷ Describe Romeo's feelings for Rosaline at the beginning of the play.

....

❸ How does the Prologue at the start of the play prepare us for what is to happen?

....

❹ How does Tybalt's seeing Romeo at the ball affect the course of the story?

....

❺ Explain the consequence of Romeo killing himself just before Juliet awakes (V.3).

....

REVISION ACTIVITY

❶ Explain why the Prince decides to punish Romeo with banishment, not death.

Start: *The Prince says (I.1) that if there is any more fighting, the guilty will be punished with death …*

❷ Pick out the ways in which chance or fate changes the course of the love affair.

Start: *Romeo and Benvolio happen to meet the Servant (I.2) who has been given the task of handing out invitations to the ball …*

GRADE BOOSTER

How do the ages of Romeo and Juliet affect the audience's understanding of their love affair?

Think about:

● Romeo's impetuousness and desire for action

● Juliet's inability to control her feelings and the openness of her nature

For a C grade: Convey your ideas clearly and appropriately (you could use words from the question to guide your answer) and refer to details from the text (use specific examples).

For an A grade: Make sure you comment on the varied ways their youthfulness comes across in the narrative, and if possible come up with your own original ideas. For example, do they take more risks because they are younger, or does their innocence make their love purer and stronger as a result?

Language

Here are a range of useful terms to know when writing about *Romeo and Juliet*, what they mean and how they occur in the play.

Literary term	Means?	Example
Dramatic irony	When the audience is aware of something about which the characters have no knowledge	Juliet is excited at the prospect of Romeo coming to her room after their marriage but is unaware that Romeo has been banished (III.2)
Sonnet	A fourteen-line poem commonly used to celebrate some aspect of love	Romeo and Juliet's first meeting is written in the form of a sonnet (I.5.93–106)
Soliloquy	A speech made when a character reveals his/her thoughts only to the audience	Romeo's first sight and first impressions of Juliet are shown in this way (I.5.44–53)
Imagery	Language used to describe characters and situations that creates mental pictures and other sense impressions	The constant references to light to describe Juliet, as exemplified by Romeo's first sight of her in the garden (II.2.2–4)
Blank verse	Unrhymed verse with each line consisting of ten syllables	'The clock struck nine when I did send the Nurse –' Juliet (II.5.1)

THE LANGUAGE CHARACTERS SPEAK

A considerable variety of language is used in *Romeo and Juliet*. As in other Shakespearean plays, the nobility mainly speak in **blank verse**, while the lower classes use **prose**. A clear illustration of this can be seen in the opening scene of the play where the servants exchange insults in prose, which gives way to blank verse when the more aristocratic members of the cast deliver their lines.

EXAMINER'S TIP: WRITING ABOUT LANGUAGE AND CLASS

In writing about Shakespeare's mixture of blank verse and prose, you could point out that the differences in expression emphasise the difference between the servants and their social superiors.

KEY CONNECTIONS

Watch Franco Zeffirelli's 1968 film version of *Romeo and Juliet*. Listen to how the actors speak their lines. Can you hear a difference between spoken blank verse and prose?

BLANK VERSE

This term does not just mean unrhymed poetry. Technically, **blank verse** consists of unrhymed **iambic pentameters**: in other words, lines with ten syllables, five of which are stressed as indicated in this line:

'Who nów the príce of hís dear blóod doth ówe?'

Shakespeare's blank verse uses this basic pattern, but he often varies it: he captures the sound of speech by changing the length and rhythm of lines.

THE FRIAR'S LANGUAGE

The Friar clearly has a high opinion of himself – one that is shared by the Nurse (III.3.158–60). He is unable to express himself briefly. He enjoys many long speeches throughout the play.

THE SOLILOQUY

Shakespeare uses the **soliloquy** to enable Juliet to 'think out loud' and reveal her deepest feelings in Act II scene 2 lines 43–9. Notice that Juliet ends her speech in the middle of the line of blank verse, with 'Take all myself' (line 49), and Romeo completes the line, picking up the word 'take' and accepting her offer. Juliet has started the line and the thought, and Romeo, acting in harmony, completes both the line and the thought: 'I take thee …'.

THE THEME OF LOVE AND THE SONNET

Shakespeare uses the **sonnet** form on a number of occasions: most obviously in the opening Prologues to Acts I and II, and more subtly at the start of Romeo and Juliet's love affair. When you look more closely at the lovers' first meeting (I.5.93–106), you will see that the first **quatrain** of the sonnet is given to Romeo, and the second to Juliet. The lovers share the next four lines and between them they compose the final couplet. It is as if each is instantly on the other's wavelength – a sure sign that they are in love!

GRADE BOOSTER

Analysing the way lines are phrased in order to convey tension is a very high-level skill.

EXAMINER'S TIP: WRITING ABOUT LOVE AND POETRY

When Shakespeare uses the **sonnet** form at the start of their love affair, notice how he shares the lines between the lovers so that they are both involved in creating this beautiful passage of poetry.

LIGHT IMAGERY

Similes and **metaphors** form part of the play's **imagery**. The continual references to sources of bright light, lightning itself, gunpowder and explosions affect the audience's imaginative responses. Romeo and Juliet are 'star-crossed lovers' (I.Prologue.6). On one level, the stars represent fate – the pair are fated to die. On another level, a star may be seen as something bright which shows up against the darkness of the night sky. What we have is a love which is brilliant but short-lived, passing across the dark face of a troubled society. In addition, the image carries with it excitement and a compelling speed of action.

JULIET'S LANGUAGE

Once you start looking for references to their love being seen as a light for the world, you will probably be amazed at how often they occur. Look at Juliet's speech when she is anxiously awaiting the arrival of Romeo on their wedding night. She wants to see him so much, but even at this moment of sheer joy she anticipates his death. Notice the words she uses which convey how she sees him: '... when I shall die, / Take him and cut him out in little stars' (III.2.21–2).

Juliet's behaviour towards the end of the balcony scene (II.2) where her meeting with Romeo is coming to an end is touching. She has to go but does not want to leave. She leaves and re-enters three times, the last time uttering memorably, 'I have forgot why I did call thee back' (line 170). This freshness and directness of expression help to make her a bewitching heroine.

It is significant that throughout the play Juliet speaks in verse, making her language always a thing of beauty.

INAPPROPRIATE USE OF POETRY

Throughout the play the poetry is used carefully, sometimes to give a sense of artificiality: the grief of the Capulets, the Nurse and Paris for the 'dead' Juliet is a notable example of this (IV.5.14–64). Their grieving seems a little unconvincing – they had, after all, driven Juliet to kill herself.

CHECKPOINT 15

Over how many days does the story take place?

Structure

The action of the story covers a period of five days: the opening street fight occurs on a Sunday morning, and by early on Thursday morning the lovers have died and the feuding families are united.

The plot revolves entirely around the lovers. We see them before they meet each other. We witness their first meeting. We follow them through their declarations of love and up to the crucial moment when Romeo kills Tybalt. We sense them fighting against time as the wedding with Paris is brought forward and the Friar tries to save them.

Inevitably, as events move so quickly, mistakes are made. The vital message fails to reach Romeo. Juliet wakes up fractionally too late to save Romeo and herself.

A CONCENTRATED STORY

The plot is a complicated one only because so many external things affect the love affair. The absence of **sub-plots** ensures that throughout the 'two hours' traffic' our attention is firmly fixed on the fate of the young lovers.

THE TIMESCALE

The fact that the story is played out over such a short period of days makes it more powerful. The lovers are caught up in a fast-moving series of events beyond their control.

THE FUTURE FORESEEN

A feature of the play is the way in which the future is anticipated, or foreshadowed. The opening Chorus is a prime example: we are told that this love story will end in the deaths of the lovers. There are several similar instances.

As Romeo and his friends are making their way to the masked ball (I.4), he tells Mercutio that he has had a dream. Mercutio's lengthy response, the Queen Mab soliloquy (lines 55–104), prevents Romeo from telling us what he had dreamed. We are left to work out what it must have been from Romeo's closing lines (107–114) where he says that he has a premonition that something terrible will happen that night. We could describe Romeo's dream as an omen.

We also note the Friar's words (II.6.9–15) where he warns that 'violent delights have violent ends'. His closing line, 'Too swift arrives as tardy as too slow', about loving too hastily, ironically predicts Romeo finding Juliet in the tomb. He arrives too early to find her awake, which is the circumstance that leads to both their deaths.

KEY QUOTE

'Get thee to church a Thursday, / Or never after look me in the face!' (III.5.160–1).

? DID YOU KNOW

Only four days have passed since Capulet said Juliet could marry whoever she liked.

EXAMINER'S TIP: WRITING ABOUT TRAGIC STRUCTURE

In writing about the play's structure, you should refer to the arc-like nature of the plot: the first two acts build up to the wedding; the remainder of the play shows what goes wrong, with the death of Tybalt leading inevitably to the final tragedy.

Progress and revision check

REVISION ACTIVITY

❶ Make a note of the occasions where a **sonnet** is used in the play. (Write your answers below)

....

❷ Show how the status of the characters determines whether prose or poetry is used in Act I scene 1.

....

❸ Pick out two occasions in Act I where Romeo uses light imagery to describe Juliet.

....

❹ What does the Friar's wordiness of expression suggest about his character?

....

❺ Pick out two soliloquies where a character reveals his or her true feelings.

....

REVISION ACTIVITY

❶ What effect does the compressed timescale have upon the story?

Start: *Everything happens so quickly in the play. No sooner has Romeo met Juliet than he is arranging to marry her …*

❷ Shakespeare uses **dramatic irony** throughout the play: pick out three occasions where it is used and explain its effect.

Start: *From the very start of the play, the audience knows that the love affair is doomed …*

GRADE BOOSTER

Look at the way Shakespeare uses **dialogue** in the balcony scene (II.2) to capture the feelings of people falling in love.

Think about:

● The opening part of the scene where each character delivers a soliloquy revealing their feelings

● Juliet's request that Romeo should swear his love for her

For a C grade: make sure you cover all the important moments in the scene (using short quotations where possible) and refer to details in the text such as Juliet's embarrassment.

For an A grade: make a general statement about what happens emotionally in the scene and then concentrate on details, such as Juliet's reluctance to leave Romeo, picking out the way her words are phrased to reveal her confused state of mind.

PART SIX: GRADE BOOSTER

Understanding the question

Questions in exams or controlled conditions often need **'decoding'**. Decoding the question helps to ensure that your answer will be relevant and refers to what you have been asked.

 ## UNDERSTAND EXAM LANGUAGE

Get used to exam and essay style language by looking at specimen questions and the words they use. For example:

Exam speak!	Means?	Example
'What do you think?'	This is asking for your opinions, backed up with evidence from the text.	Showing the Friar gathering herbs might convey that these will be important later in the play
'The methods Shakespeare uses'	How he shows us what we are meant to think about a character.	By contrasting happy and sad events Shakespeare uses a technique called pathos, e.g. Juliet takes the potion as her wedding is prepared elsewhere
'How does the writer portray ...?'	How does the writer give us a mind's eye picture of a character or an event?	Shakespeare presents the story as an event that has already happened, to represent the power of fate

 ## 'BREAK DOWN' THE QUESTION

Pick out the **key words** or phrases. For example:

> **Question:** 'Why does **Juliet change** her attitude towards the **Nurse**?'

- Focus on the **effect** of the Nurse's **behaviour** on Juliet, e.g. the way the *Nurse* changes her attitude to Romeo once he is banished

- The words 'change her attitude' invite you to look at Juliet's character **development**.

What does this tell you?

- **Focus** on the Nurse's advice to Juliet to forget Romeo and choose Paris for a husband, the effect this has on Juliet, and how Juliet's attitude changes.

 ## KNOW YOUR LITERARY LANGUAGE!

When studying texts, you will come across words such as 'theme', 'irony', 'sonnet' and 'metaphor'. Some of these words could come up in questions you are asked. MAKE SURE you know what they mean before you use them!

Planning your answer

It is vital that you plan your response to the controlled assessment task or possible exam question carefully, and that you then follow your plan, if you are to gain the higher grades.

 Do the research!

When revising for the exam, or planning your response to the controlled assessment task, collect **evidence** (for example, quotations) that will support what you have to say. For example, if preparing to answer a question on how Shakespeare has explored the theme of dutiful love you might list ideas as follows:

Key point	Evidence/quotation	Act/scene/line, etc.
Paris's love for Juliet is strong: he comes to lay flowers at her grave and to mourn her death on the night they were due to be married.	'Sweet flower, with flowers thy bridal bed I strew'	Act V scene 3 line 12

PLAN FOR PARAGRAPHS

Use paragraphs to plan your answer. For example:

❶ The first paragraph should **introduce** the **argument** you wish to make.

❷ Then, jot down how the paragraphs that follow will **develop** this argument. Include **details**, **examples** and other possible **points of view**. Each paragraph is likely to deal with one point at a time.

❸ Sum up your argument in the last paragraph.

For example, for the following task:

Question: How does Shakespeare present the character of Lord Capulet? Comment on the language devices and techniques used.

Simple plan:

- Paragraph 1: *Introduction*, e.g. Say who Capulet is and what role he plays.
- Paragraph 2: *First point*, e.g. Capulet calls for his sword to join in the fighting in Act I scene 1.
- Paragraph 3: *Second point*, e.g. He is keen to let Juliet choose her husband.
- Paragraph 4: *Third point*, e.g. Later he is determined that Juliet will marry Paris.
- Paragraph 5: *Fourth point*, e.g. He finally realises the futility of the family feud.
- Paragraph 6: *Conclusion*, e.g. Sum up the character of Capulet and how Shakespeare presents him.

How to use quotations

One of the secrets of success in writing essays is to use quotations **effectively**. There are five basic principles:

❶ Put inverted commas, i.e. ' ', around the quotation.

❷ Write the quotation exactly as it appears in the original.

❸ Do not use a quotation that repeats what you have just written.

❹ Use the quotation so that it fits into your sentence.

❺ Only quote what is most useful.

TOP ✓ TIP USE QUOTATIONS TO DEVELOP YOUR ARGUMENT

Quotations should be used to develop the line of thought in your essays. Your comment should not duplicate what is in your quotation. For example:

GRADE D	GRADE C
(simply repeats the idea)	(makes a point and supports it with a relevant quotation)
Prince Escalus says that the families have caused public brawls three times before: 'Three civil brawls bred of an airy word [...] Have thrice disturbed the quiet of our streets ...' (I.1.83–5)	We can see that the family conflict is deep-rooted as the Prince condemns the families for having 'Three civil brawls'.

However, the most sophisticated way of using the writer's words is to embed them into your sentence, and further develop the point:

GRADE A

(makes point, embeds quote and develops idea)

Family conflict is clearly deep-rooted. What most seems to infuriate the Prince is that this is the third of the 'civil brawls' that he has been obliged to break up, which may also make us wonder how hot-headed and violent Verona is as a city under his command.

When you use quotations in this way, you are demonstrating the ability to use text as evidence to support your ideas – not simply including words from the original to prove you have read it.

EXAMINER'S TIP

Try using a quotation to begin your response. You can use it as a launch-pad for your ideas, or as an idea you are going to argue against.

Sitting the examination

Examination papers are carefully designed to give you the opportunity to do your best. Follow these handy hints for exam success:

 BEFORE YOU START

- Make sure that you **know the texts** you are writing about so that you are properly prepared and equipped.
- You need to be **comfortable** and **free from distractions**. Inform the invigilator if anything is off-putting, e.g. a shaky desk.
- **Read** and follow the instructions, or rubric, on the front of the examination paper. You should know by now what you need to do but **check** to reassure yourself.
- Before beginning your answer, have a **skim** through the **whole paper** to make sure you don't miss anything **important**.
- Observe the **time allocation** – and follow it carefully. If they recommend 45 minutes for a particular question on a text make sure this is how long you spend.

 **EXAMINER'S TIP**

Prepare for the exam/ assessment! Whatever you need to bring, make sure you have it with you – books, if you're allowed, pens, pencils – and that you turn up on time!

 WRITING YOUR RESPONSES

A typical 45 minutes examination essay is probably between 550 and 800 words in length.

Ideally, spend a minimum of 5 minutes planning your answer before you begin.

Use the questions to structure your response. Here is an example:

Question: Do you see the ending of the play as negative or positive?

- The introduction to your answer could briefly describe **the ending** of the play;
- the second part could explain what could be seen as **positive**;
- the third part could be an exploration of the **negative** aspects;
- the conclusion would **sum up your own viewpoint**.

For each part allocate paragraphs to cover the points you wish to make (see **Planning your answer**).

Keep your writing clear and easy to read, using paragraphs and link words to show the structure of your answers.

Spend a couple of minutes afterwards quickly checking for obvious errors.

TOP TIP **'KEY WORDS' ARE THE KEY!**

Keep on mentioning the **key words** from the question in your answer. This will keep you on track and remind the examiner that you are answering the question set.

Sitting the controlled assessment

It may be the case that you are responding to *Romeo and Juliet* in a controlled assessment situation. Follow these useful tips for success.

 ## KNOW WHAT YOU ARE REQUIRED TO DO

Make sure you are clear about:

- The **specific text** and **task** you are preparing (is it on just *Romeo and Juliet*, or more than one text?)
- How **long** you have during the assessment period (i.e. 3–4 hours?)
- How **much** you are expected or allowed to write (i.e. 2,000 words?)
- **What** you are **allowed to take** into the controlled assessment, and what you can use (or not, as the case may be!) You may be able to take in brief notes BUT NOT draft answers, so check with your teacher.

KNOW HOW YOU CAN PREPARE

Once you know your task, topic and text/s you can:

- Make **notes** and **prepare** the **points**, **evidence**, **quotations**, etc. you are likely to use.
- Practise or draft **model answers**.
- Use these **York Notes** to hone your **skills**, e.g. use of quotations, how to plan an answer and focus on what makes a **top grade**.

IN THE CONTROLLED ASSESSMENT

Remember:

- **Stick** to the topic and task you have been given.
- The allocated **time** is for **writing**, so make the most of it. It is **double** the time you might have in an exam, so you will be writing almost **twice as much** (or more).
- **If** you are **allowed** access to a **dictionary or thesaurus** make use of them; if not, don't go near them!
- At the end of the controlled assessment follow your **teacher's instructions**. For example, make sure you have written your **name** clearly on all the pages you hand in.

GRADE BOOSTER

Where appropriate, refer to the language technique used by the writer and the effect it creates. For example, if you say 'this metaphor shows how ...', or 'the effect of this metaphor is to emphasise to the reader ...', this could get you higher marks.

Improve your grade

It is useful to know the type of responses examiners are looking for when they award different grades. The following broad guidance should help you to improve your grade when responding to the task you are set!

GRADE C

What you need to show	What this means
Sustained response to task and text	You write enough! You don't run out of ideas after two paragraphs.
Effective use of **details** to **support your explanations**	You generally support what you say with evidence, e.g. The Nurse betrays Juliet when she says, 'I think it best you married with the County.'
Explanation of the writer's **use of language, structure, form**, etc., and the **effect on readers**	You must write about the writer's use of these things. It's not enough simply to give a viewpoint. So, you might comment on the lovers' first words at the masked ball being written in sonnet form.
Appropriate comment on **characters, plot, themes, ideas** and **settings**	What you say is relevant. If the task asks you to comment on how Benvolio is a natural peacemaker, you might describe his attempts to stop the fighting in the first scene of the play.

GRADE A

What you need to show *in addition* to the above	What this means
Insightful, exploratory response to the text	You look beyond the obvious. You might question the reason behind the Friar agreeing to marry Romeo and Juliet by considering his motives.
Close analysis and use of **detail**	If you are looking at the writer's use of language, you comment on each word in a sentence, drawing out its distinctive effect on the reader, e.g. 'Thy beauty hath made me effeminate,' the words Romeo uses to question his masculinity when he refuses to duel with Tybalt in Act III scene 1.
Convincing and **imaginative interpretation**	Your viewpoint is likely to convince the examiner. You show you have *engaged* with the text, and come up with your own ideas. These may be based on what you have discussed in class or read about, but you have made your own decisions.

Annotated sample answers

This section will provide you with extracts from **two model answers**, one at **C grade** and one at **A grade**, to give you an idea of what is required to **achieve** different levels.

> **Question:** Read Capulet's speeches in Act I scene 2 lines 7–34. Answer both parts of the question.
>
> ● How does Shakespeare present Capulet's thoughts and feelings about Juliet?
>
> ● How does Shakespeare present a different view of his relationship with Juliet later in the play?

CANDIDATE 1

Neatly sums up the gist of the scene

In this scene Capulet is discussing with Paris if Capulet is prepared to let Juliet marry him. Capulet seems quite pleased, especially since Paris is related to the Prince of Verona, though he has a few objections. He tells Paris that his daughter is a bit young since she is not yet fourteen and he would rather she waited till she was a couple of years older, 'Let two more summers wither in their pride / Ere we may think her ripe to be a bride.'

Identifies his main objection

Does not cross refer to Lady Capulet

Paris says that lots of girls her age are already mothers, 'happy mothers made'. Capulet says lots of girls are not happy at being married so young but he can see that Paris is still keen, so he says Paris is welcome to come to an 'old accustomed feast' he is having that night. If he fancies Juliet, he can 'woo her'. As her father he won't stand in her way if he can 'get her heart'.

Capulet comes across as a kind man who wants the best for his daughter.

Rather weak

Later in the play, we see a different side of Capulet. In Act III scene 4, Paris has returned the day after the ball to see if Capulet will now agree to the marriage. He has not had time to ask if Juliet does fancy Paris but he says he is sure she will go along with the plan. 'I think she will be ruled / In all respects by me.'

Quotation not very well integrated

Capulet does not want to hang around so suggests that the marriage should take place on Thursday, in three days' time. Paris replies that he wishes they could get married tomorrow.

Could make reference here to structure of play

Naturally when he goes to tell Juliet of the arrangement, she is far from happy and Capulet loses his temper. He tells her in Act III scene 5 that if she refuses to marry the man he has chosen, 'so worthy a gentleman', then he will drag her to the church 'on a hurdle'. If that doesn't work, she can leave his house and as far as he is concerned can 'die in the streets'.

Good supporting quote

In the space of two days, he has turned into a completely different father!

Neat strong ending

This is a sound piece of writing supported with apt quotations. The candidate has stayed quite close to the order of events as they come in the text. The details of the conversations are faithfully recorded and there is much valid comment. The essay fails to consider wider issues such as where the arranged marriage fits into the dramatic structure of the play.

GRADE C

CANDIDATE 2

Neat summary of the scene

In this scene Capulet is discussing with Paris the possibility of his marrying Juliet. Paris is quite a good catch: he is rich and well-connected, a 'kinsman of the Prince'. Nevertheless, Capulet is quite protective about his daughter since she is still 'a stranger in the world' being not yet fourteen. This is not an insurmountable obstacle to marriage. After all, in the very next scene we learn that Lady Capulet was already a mother by Juliet's age.

Excellent interpretation

Capulet realises that Paris will not be put off by his objections so invites him to 'an old accustomed feast' at his house that night, where all the most beautiful young women of Verona will be on show. There he will be able to compare Juliet with all the 'fresh female buds' and if he likes her and she is agreeable to a marriage, then he will not stand in her way.

Well-handled quote

We quite like Capulet after this. After all, he is not one of those manipulating fathers who will force his daughter into a relationship she does not want.

Strong evidence of personal response

An entirely different Capulet bursts onto the scene after the death of Tybalt. When Paris returns the day after the ball to see what Juliet's verdict on him has been, Capulet brushes aside any thought that she might object and fixes the marriage three days ahead. In fact, if it had been possible, he would have had the marriage even earlier, so convinced is he that she would be 'ruled in all respects' by him.

Excellent observation

When he communicates the arrangement to Juliet, she is horrified and in Act III scene 5, he is furious at her refusal to bow to his will and threatens to throw her out onto the streets.

Powerful language captures Capulet's mood

Thus in the space of two short days, Capulet has descended from being a kind, tolerant father to being a complete monster. This has two effects on the play: it makes Juliet desperate to find any remedy to avoid marrying Paris; and it forces the pace of the play to the point where the Friar has to come out with far-fetched plans in order to save Juliet – and his own skin!

Original and powerful

Widens the significance of the scene

This is an excellent essay which gives clear evidence of a personal response, where observations are supported with quotations that are handled in a mature manner. Instead of dwelling on explanation, the candidate has summarised the **dialogue** and used this to make wider points about the significance of this part of the plot to the play as a whole.

GRADE A

Further questions

CONTROLLED ASSESSMENT-STYLE QUESTIONS

For the controlled assessment candidates are required to produce work of about 2,000 words in a period of up to 4 hours.

❶ Explore the ways in which divisions in society are shown in the stage version of *Romeo and Juliet* and in one or more film versions, e.g. by Franco Zeffirelli and/or Baz Luhrmann.

❷ Write about the ways that two central characters, such as Romeo and Juliet or the Friar and the Nurse, are presented and developed in the play and compare and contrast this with the ways in which they are handled in a film version of the text.

❸ Consider the effect that choice of setting has upon *Romeo and Juliet*. In your writing, use the play as your starting-point and make comparisons with one or more film versions.

❹ Write about Shakepeare's use of language and dramatic devices in handling the love story of *Romeo and Juliet*, and show how another writer from the English Literary Heritage has used different or similar techniques in presenting a different love story.

❺ Explore the way interpretations of Shakespeare change over time by comparing two or more film or audio versions of the play.

EXAM-STYLE QUESTIONS

❶ Read Act I scene 2

What do you think of the way Capulet and Paris speak and behave here? Then look at their second meeting in Act III scene 4. What changes do you note in what they say and do? Remember to support your answer with words and phrases from the extract.

❷ Read Act I scene 5

In what ways does Shakespeare make Romeo and Juliet's first meeting so effective? Compare this first scene with one later in the play that shows a different side to their relationship.

❸ Look at Act I scene 1

Explain how the families' feuding is represented. Then consider Act III scene 1 and show the ways in which neither side has learnt from their earlier errors. In what ways do the consequences of the scenes differ?

❹ Read the Friar's lines 1–42 (II.3)

In what ways are the Friar's thoughts and feelings about himself represented? How does he come across in the views of others later in the play?

❺ Read Act I scene 3

Show how Shakespeare reveals the close friendship between the Nurse and Juliet. By clear reference to the text later in the play, explain how this friendship comes to an end.

LITERARY TERMS

Literary term	Explanation
antithesis	a figure of speech in which thoughts are balanced in contrast
atmosphere	a mood or feeling
aubade	a sunrise song or poem
blank verse	unrhymed **iambic pentameter**
character(s)	either a person in a play, novel, etc., or his or her personality
confidant(e)	a close male (female) friend entrusted with secrets
couplet	a pair of rhymed lines of any metre
denouement	the climax of a play
dialogue	a conversation between two or more characters; or the words spoken by characters in general
dramatic device	a trick or technique used by the playwright to make the play more effective, such as **dramatic irony** (see below)
dramatic irony	when the audience knows more about what is happening than some of the characters
iambic pentameter	a line of poetry consisting of five iambic feet
imagery	descriptive language which uses images to make actions, objects and characters more vivid in the reader's mind – **metaphors** and **similes** are examples of imagery
irony	when someone deliberately says one thing when they mean another, usually in a humorous or sarcastic way
metaphor	when one thing is used to describe another thing to create a striking or unusual image
narrative	a story or tale and the particular way that it is told
oxymoron	when contradictory terms are brought together
pathos	the depiction of events in a way that evokes strong feelings of pity or sorrow in the reader
petrarchan love	a type of love described by the Italian poet Petrarch (1307–74), where a man worships a lady from afar
quatrain	a verse of poetry four lines in length
rhythm	in poetry or music, the pattern of stresses or beats in a line
simile	when one thing is compared directly to another thing, using the words 'like' or 'as'
soliloquy	when a character speaks directly to the audience as if thinking aloud, revealing their inner thoughts, feelings and intentions
sonnet	a poem of fourteen lines generally concerned with a single thought
setting	the scene of a play
sub-plot	a story concerning minor characters in a play
theme	a recurrent idea in a work of literature
tragedy	a drama dealing with tragic events
vocabulary	the language used, e.g. the words chosen by the writer

CHECKPOINT ANSWERS

CHECKPOINT 1

That he is always looking for trouble.

CHECKPOINT 2

By comparing her with other beautiful women at the ball.

CHECKPOINT 3

Why does he have to have that name.

CHECKPOINT 4

He is surprised because he thought Romeo loved Rosaline.

CHECKPOINT 5

Because she will not directly tell her Romeo's plans.

CHECKPOINT 6

Because he is a 'kinsman to the Montagues'.

CHECKPOINT 7

That she has an image of him lying in a tomb.

CHECKPOINT 8

Because she now agrees to marry Paris.

CHECKPOINT 9

That Juliet is dead and lying in the Capulet family vault.

CHECKPOINT 10

The Prince says he still has repect for him, 'a holy man'.

CHECKPOINT 11

They are cousins.

CHECKPOINT 12

She had looked after Juliet since she was a baby.

CHECKPOINT 13

Because he is wealthy and related to the Prince.

CHECKPOINT 14

Four times (I.5, II.2, II.3, III.5).

CHECKPOINT 15

Four and a half.